C-Gate 6

In Loving Memory of My Brother Alan

Special thanks to:

Sandra Mueller

Nelda (Thelma) Butler

Rose Letherby

Diana Williams-Liaeff

Cover art by: Russ Meinka

Chapter 1

C-gate 1

The night was chilled, it reminded Yoman of his childhood, growing up in the Electric District near Haybanks Mississippi. He was standing outside the mansion, his eyes following the trails of the launches as they left Earth.

The sky was clear tonight while Yoman watched the lights in the house turn on, then turn off, from room to room. He wondered if he was tracking a resident or a servant. Standing outside, impatiently waiting to be brought in through the front security gate. Head lights approached from both directions of the street, making him a little antsy. Standing in front of the Governor's Mansion the last thing he needed was to be seen by anyone, even if it was just a passerby.

Right on schedule the little red light turned green and then with a hum and a beep the heavy duty black wrought iron gate started its rattling journey down the steel track, stopping with a musical twang and a clank. The governor's limo exited the property giving Yoman just enough time to slip through before the oncoming traffic arrived.

A whistle could be heard coming from the shadows just beyond the lights. Like dutiful sentries a row of lamp posts illuminated the driveway. Kester Trewer the thirty five year old only son of the governor stepped out of the din and into the light so Yoman could see him. Kester was once a good looking young man, toasted by many as the most eligible bachelor of the area. This was, however, no longer the case. Years of his father's political agenda and his mother's suicide left him neglected, alone and depressed. He spent the last ten of those years becoming a junky. He succeeded to the fullest.

He and his life became an unspoken diary within his father's political circles. From time to time people were employed to keep an eye on him and to keep the press quiet. This, added to the cost of his habit, sung to a tune of over two million dollars over the course of the last ten years.

Casually the two men walked up the driveway and entered the house through the poolside doors. Kester was hoping for a night of heavy drinking and the latest designer drugs.

Yoman was looking out the window watching the ripples in the pool. The floral scent of the water was easy on his senses. Kester reached around him from behind and handed him a drink in a cobalt blue glass and asked with a slight tremble in his voice, no doubt due to withdrawals. "When is Porter gonna show up?"

Yoman looked at Kester and with an evil smile on his face he said, "I told you man, as soon as I'm sure your old man is on that shuttle and the risk of getting arrested again is gone. Then you'll get your precious little boost." His smile waned and his eyes glared over, he turned his back to Kester and raised his voice a little speaking towards the wall. "I gave up four years of my life because the Governors brat kid is a junkie and Porter got to walk." He took a sip of his drink, turned back to face Kester and continued. "Bunch of losers you, your old man and Porter, the whole lot of you worthless."

Kester hung his head as a blanket of hatred washed over him. He opened his mouth to scream at Yoman when the buzzer on the wall alerted them that Porter arrived and the night was about to begin.

The red light on the monitor turned green as the heavy gate made its second journey down the track for the night, letting another person onto the property.

Sweat was beginning to bead up on Kester's forehead, his hands became unsteady but he knew before he got his high on, he had to remove the security tapes from the monitoring console. He figured he would deal with his father another day. Little did he know, another day was not in his future, at least according to Yoman's plan.

Yoman –The man

Yoman born Francis Bain Lewis. The third and last child, his parents were less than interested in raising him. Starving for affection and fighting for status in the Electric District, it was no surprise to anyone, he would end up on the tracks doing hard labor. It was, however, quite a surprise that he would graduate from the academy with honors and with a degree in Zero Gravity Engineering and Plumbing.

Known on the job as Frank Lewis. He was a skinny little man, missing most of his teeth with an inferiority complex and an ego that cost him the love and respect from not only his own family but from everyone who he had ever come into contact with. Somewhere however, he must have friends in high places to have been given the honor to be part of Quincy 4's last journey.

Being a member of the disposal company, Lewis was privileged to a few unique opportunities not offered to the general public. Most of which are illegal on Earth but since space itself falls under no specific jurisdiction, Earth laws don't really mean much, unless of course you get caught on Earth. His credit was good enough to obtain anything he needed or wanted including the latest designer drugs. Lewis could not afford to have his license revoked on Earth for engaging in any illegal activities; so for the price of cheap dope, he left that job up to Porter.

Porter, a real scum bag of a man, standing tall at six foot five inches, long black curly hair so full of grease he combed it back without effort. Born with his left leg three inches shorter than his right, always gave him the advantage in every situation he found himself in. People either feared him or pitied him but either way he used it to his advantage to accomplish whatever deviant plan he had in the works. When he walked he would lift his left leg high in the air and his club foot would fall to the ground with a resounding thud. Often times he exaggerated this walk just for attention. His smile was just as grotesque as his charm and strangely enough he was almost always in the company of gorgeous women.

Kester paced the floor of the south den anxiously awaiting Porter's arrival. He walked to the window and pretended to be staring at the soft reflection of light in the pool, without turning his head to face Lewis and Porter.

"Hey Porter," he said as his voice cracked. His throat was dry and starting to close up on him. He struggled just to get those two words out of his mouth.

Porter turned from his conversation with Yoman and asked, "What is it, that's so important that you needed to interrupt my business deal?"

Kester winced, Yoman snickered, and Porter turned his back to Kester again and resumed his conversation.

To witness a junkie going through withdrawals can be likened to nothing else you have ever seen before. Kester was getting more desperate with the passing of every second. His face turned pale and his knuckles were white as sheets. His throat was now almost all the way closed and the light was starting to hurt his eyes. Soaked in sweat, shaking from head to toe, he squinted his eyes to keep a bead on Porter. He approached the foul smelling giant of a man, grabbed him by the arm and spun him around. A move which took all three men by surprise.

"Don't turn your back on me when I'm talking to you," Kester squeaked. His eyes were mere slits, his desperation and anger streaking across his face like a lightning bolt. He struggled to keep from falling over.

Porter grinned at Kester's attempt to be a man. Yoman put his hand inside his jacket and took a few unnoticeable steps backwards. Kester, somewhere found the muster to place a hand around Porter's throat. "I need boosted now," barely audible he said with breath belching like a hot fire.

Porter effortlessly spun to his right causing Kester's hand to drop from his neck and fall to his side. With a slight shove from Porter, Kester found himself on the floor. Half under the game table and half looking like a passed out drunk. He urinated himself then started to cry.

Porter was now starting to feel the effects of needing to get high too. He turned towards Yoman expecting to see a baggie of drugs, then froze. Instead, he was met with the barrel of Yoman's pistol pointed right at his head. Terror washed over his face, not so much because he had a gun pointed at him. It wasn't the first time in his crummy existence. He was terrified because his pistol was in his long black leather coat which was draped over the game table on the other side of the room.

"Hold on a sec Yoman," Porter grimaced. "You going to kill me?"

Yoman just smiled and gave a subtle nod.

"Why?! I did everything you asked." His voice sounded like he was going through puberty again.

Yoman walked closer. "Do you know why they call me Yoman?" his voice was flat, his tone was curt.

Porter could only manage to shake his head no. Yoman asked the question again only this time he raised the volume in his voice and at the same time cocked the trigger on his pistol. "N-n-n-o-o-o why d-do th-th-they call you Yo-oman." He raised his arms above his head and held a hand out in front of his face like he was trying block the bullet. He started to whimper, if the fear didn't kill him soon the lack of drugs surely will.

Meantime Kester managed to raise himself to a slouched position against the leg of his game table. He watched through swollen eyes and listened as Yoman's answer thundered through his head. Each word seemingly getting louder than the last, pounding themselves like a rusty nail into his aching head.

Yoman placed the barrel of his gun against Porter's forehead and began to speak. His words were articulate and bold, his voice was loud and strong. Like a street corner preacher he delivered the last words Porter would ever hear.

"They call me Yoman, beeee-cause," he paused for effect. "Beeee-cause when I got sentenced to work the tracks for four years, I was the Yoman. Yoman get me this, Yoman get me that, Yoman find this tool, Yoman bring me water." By now his face was a furious red color, his teeth were clenched. "Yoman this and Yoman that," he reached the pinnacle of his tirade and then lowered his voice to ask Porter one final question.

"Do you remember?" He pressed the gun barrel harder into Porter's forehead. "Why I was sentenced to four years on the track?" He pushed Porter's head back with his gun so their eyes could meet. "Because I was set up. Set up by you!"

Porter opened his mouth to try to defend himself and at that very instant his brains became part of the decorum on the glass pool doors. Yoman never flinched, he walked over to Kester and tossed him a baggie full of dope. "What a whimpering priss he turned out to be." Chuckling he looked down at Kester. "Get your act together and do it fast, we don't have much time."

Kester, now able to function somewhat, started screaming in terror at Yoman.

"What did you just do man?!" He put his hands on his head and started to pace in a circle. His tremors had started to ease up while his mind was trying to digest the dead body lying on the floor of the south den at 4335 West Polk Rd, his home and the Governor's mansion.

Yoman knew time was no longer on his side. He handed Kester his gun. "Here hold this while I find something to wrap this dead scum bucket in."

Without thinking Kester took the gun from Yoman's steady hand and walked over to the glass doors leading out to the pool. All he could manage to do was stare at the blood and brains as they ran down the smooth surface of the glass. He opened the baggie and took another hit of dope. Ten minutes later he threw up all over the door adding vomit and his DNA to an already grotesque crime scene.

As his shaking started to stop, he said, "I can't believe you just killed Porter."

His voice now returning to its normal pitch. Yoman turned to Kester, smiled and in a low, even slightly condescending tone asked, "What?" He looked Kester in the eye, "Who killed Porter?" He was standing there with a plastic shower curtain in his hand. He draped it over the dead body, tucked it under Porter's left side and rolled him up like a chicken wrap.

Kester had a quizzical look on his face and justifiably so. He asked Yoman again, "Why did you have to kill him?"

Yoman stopped what he was doing and with fire burning from his eyes, he turned to Kester. With his teeth clenched and the stench of booze on his breath he growled. "I…" he took a step forward, "did not kill anyone."

His words were timed for effect. "Let's get something straight my friend. I did not kill anyone. You on the other hand have your finger prints all over the murder weapon and motive. As far as anyone else is concerned, I never set foot one on this property tonight."

Kester looked down at the gun in his hand and dropped it on the floor.

"Wh-a-a-a-t?" he stammered and started to dry heave.

"You must be joking, you're crazy, totally insane, you can't pin this on me."

Yoman was sealing up the shower curtain then with one quick jerk he lifted the body onto his shoulder. He spoke coldly and matter of factly. "Not only can I, I did. We have about twenty minutes before your daddy's driver returns so give me a hand with this."

Kester said. "You're on your own now man, I'm doing squat."

Yoman dropped the body on the floor with a sickening thud and opened the sliding glass doors, dislodging some of Porter's brains in doing so. "Alright by me," he laughed as he started to walk around the swimming pool to the row of garage doors.

Kester panicked. He dashed out the door and danced in front of Yoman. "Why man? Why did you do this and why pin it on me?" His voice was starting to crack again.

"Because I need your help and now that you know this can be traced back to you, I'm guessing you're willing to give me a hand." Yoman said with a grunt, lifting the body from the shoulders and neck, nodding to Kester to do the same at the dead man's feet.

The privilege of living in a mansion with a ten car garage had left Kester years ago. Tonight he knew it was gone for good. No chance to return to the comfort of his father's empire.

"You have keys to any of these cars?" Yoman asked Kester.

"What about the mess in my house?" Kester retorted back.

Yoman paid little attention to the question.

"Keys," he barked.

Kester jumped and pointed to an open lock box on the wall. "Looks like Bill left the box opened so take your pick of any vehicle here."

Yoman chose the least suspicious car, a three door runabout, and with the rear suspension sagging, he pulled out onto the street and silently whirred through the night. You could smell the fear on Kester as the men made the two hour trek to the sweeps dock. Yoman drove smart the whole way, calm and collected. The silence was deafening.

The electric limo silently funneled its way into the red lane at the shuttle port. The large turnabout rotated slowly with ease, this made the transition from limo to shuttle station effortless. Before he stepped out of the car, he gave William specific instructions regarding Kester, how much credit to give him and to retrieve the security tapes. "Kester never really thinks things through, does he?" He quipped to William as he tipped his hat and briskly got lost in the masses. Governor Trewer made his way into the port with his baggage following behind him on a remote controlled cart.

The day turned out to be a nice warm sunny day on Earth. William put the limo in drive, mumbled under his breath, "no, he really doesn't think things through does he". Pulled into the stream of traffic and headed back to the Governor's mansion for where he hoped he would be able to enjoy some free time.

Governor Trewer was headed for the annual global summit. No longer held on Earth due to past riots and protests. The summits are now held on C-gate 2 which is a two week journey by shuttle. He hated shuttle trips and likened them to having one of several strains of flu. No transport shuttle ever had problems during launch and re-entry, with a success rate of one hundred percent, his safety never seemed to be an issue. What he didn't like about it was pulling ten G's at launch and the fact he felt like he had to make small talk with the rest of the dignitaries on his flight.

His VIP steward met him as soon as he walked through the detection gates. For his security, he was swiftly whisked away bypassing the screening boards. The steward led him to the large heavy doors that held passage to the VIP boarding gates. He swept an arm in a flowing motion, speaking perfect English he said "This way Mr. Governor, the rest of your party is waiting in suite B".

The Governor stepped past the steward and said, "Late again." He smiled and thanked his steward before adding, "as usual," then walked through the wood grained doors that displayed the logo for The Three Day Shuttle Company. Stepping into the VIP lounge, he nodded hello to the other heads of state and dignitaries who were gathered for the summit. Sheepishly grinning as his eyes were met with some smiles, some expressionless glares and a couple cross looks, departure was waiting on him.

"My apologies," he said and took his seat.

A female voice filled the lounge saying, "departure in five minutes, please secure all loose items and fasten your harnesses. Thank you for traveling with The Three Day Shuttle Company and enjoy your stay on C-gate 2."

The Three Day Shuttle Company is the oldest and wealthiest of all the shuttle companies. Owning all of the commercial track and twenty percent of passenger and recreational track, it is the largest employer on the planet. The company also owns the dubious title of the largest prison on the planet. Not a prison of concrete and steel but a prison of labor. Small time criminals and those hard core criminals close to release are all sentenced to work the rails. So in a sense The Three Day Shuttle Company achieved most of its wealth and status from the backs and blood of the world's criminal system.

Having transport track numbering in the tens of thousands of miles worldwide and an endless supply of cheap labor, the company created a travel system to and from all points on Earth and in Earth's orbit that has remained unmatched.

Electromagnetic technology was first used sparingly in the twentieth century. Then seemed to have been put on the back burner for another hundred years. The harnessing of this technology and power became common place and inexpensive on a small scale. Just about everything now was run on some variation of electromagnetic property. The track or rails as some refer to it, operate on a large high voltage scale. Each shuttle was outfitted with several large solenoid electromagnets on the exterior while the rails were fitted with electromagnets faced in the opposite direction. Positive and negative charged impulses would silently lift the shuttle off the ground about three feet and hold it in place. Once the angle was shifted and the magnets became vertical instead of horizontal the shuttle would start to move on what seemed to be a cushion of air. As the solenoids would rotate from negative to positive, the vehicle would start its journey down the track. In theory, this type of energy could produce an infinite acceleration. Fortunately for us on Earth we neither had the land mass or materials for that scale of speed. However, in just a short period of seventy five years, the engineers of The Three Day Shuttle Company figured out a way to break Earth's gravitational pull with this technology. Shortly after that, this method became the standard in space launches before it became a world law. No more would the wasted energy of Earth's natural resources be used to launch another vehicle into space. Reaching Earth's orbit in this manner was like tossing a ball into the air and having it caught by some unseen force and holding it there.

Governor Trewer always said the three minute launch from Earth to orbit was the most terrifying three minutes he ever experienced. He loathed every launch he was subjected to and missed the days when a summit could be held on Earth without chaos.

The female voice once again filled the room. "Launch will commence in three, two, one." The shuttle rose above the ground quietly and smoothly then slowly moved forward before picking up speed at such a rate if you blinked you could miss the whole launch. The Governor always snickered about man's first mode of transportation, the old coal and wood burning steam locomotives of four centuries past when it was thought, if man traveled faster than twenty five miles per hour it would kill them. Twenty five miles an hour was not even a drop in the bucket of the one hundred twenty thousand miles per hour required to reach orbit. And by the time he finished that thought the shuttle reached the thirty seven degree angle five mile high launch rail and was projected into the nothingness of Earth's atmosphere on its way to orbit.

Once in orbit, The Governor retreated to his personal berth designed with VIP's in mind for hibernation as it was playfully called among short distance travelers. Hibernation consisted of all the food and drink you wanted with complete solitude. The choice not to be in the company of the other heads of state or dignitaries was not really the issue. The real issue was forming an alliance with two or three others before the summit started. Needless to say, hibernation was the preferred way to settle in for the next two weeks.

His traveling quarters were a bit cozy: but, oh, so plush and accommodating. Decorated in soft blue tones with all amenities a short distance traveler could ask for, including a wet bar hidden under the sink. He pulled up the electronic library to see if he wanted to read anything while soaking in his personal sauna. He had resolved himself to settle in, completely unaware of the events that had taken place in his home.

Back on Earth

After two hours of uncomfortable silence, Yoman turned off the highway on to Service Road West and drove on.

"This is the dump, I thought you had to be an employee to get in here?" Kester numbly stated the question.

Yoman said nothing and continued to drive.

"This is restricted area Yoman," Kester said this time with a little more urgency to his tone.

Yoman pulled up to the large blue metal gates, he turned to Kester and said, "sit up straight, smile and wave to the guard; and, by this time tomorrow you'll be explaining to the police how you were not home when the break in occurred and you have no idea whose brains are splattered all over your south den." Yoman leaned out the window and punched some numbers on a black key pad and the blue gates slowly swung open. He pulled through and stopped the car at the guard shack.

"Good afternoon Marcus," he spoke in a friendly familiar tone to the man in the booth. "How's the wife and kids?"

"Just fine Mr. Lewis, doing just fine. And how are you this afternoon sir?"

"Well outside of the fact I'll be making the last trip to C-gate 6, I would say if it got any better I'd have to charge you money for the rest of the story."

"You're part of the honored crew on that last Quincy 4 mission?" Marcus asked with a sour look on his face.

"She's been a good ship and it's gonna to be a rough trip but someone's gotta do it" Yoman answered then added, "I'll bring you some of that chocolate they make at Gate 3 on the return trip." Yoman smiled and gave a two finger salute to Marcus as the red and white striped crossing gates went up. Marcus leaned forward to try to get a glimpse of who Yoman's guest was but the car pulled away too quickly then disappeared down the mile long black top road leading up to the dump platform.

Once on the road to the dump site Yoman pulled the runabout to the side of the road and turned his attention to his stoned passenger. "No one here calls me Yoman, ever, including you, you got that?"

Kester managed a cynical smile while questions started flashing through his confused mind.

"From this point forward you call me Mr. Lewis or Frank. Don't call me Francis (which was the name on his security level badge) or Yoman. If you do I'll dump your dope along with that piece of trash in the trunk. Understand?" Having said that, he figured a stoned Kester would be easier to manage so he handed him a second bag of dope which acted as a suggestion for Kester to indulge in taking more. He did not disappoint. Tossed another high dosage capsule in his mouth and swallowed without the assistance of a drink. Absent mindedly clenching the baggie of dope tight in his fist, he just sat there staring out the windshield. Frank opened the communications box to the sweeps deck and rang up Shooster's number.

The sweeps deck was the place the garbage trucks dumped their loads. Pile after huge pile of garbage would accumulate during the week. More so during the week just prior to launch. It was Rick Shooster's job to push the piles into the awaiting barge. The deck itself measured over one million square feet. The barge sat below it and it was Shooster who spent eight hours a day Monday through Friday pushing and then sweeping the garbage down the five degree decline where it would fall over the edge landing in the barge. His tractor which he nicknamed *The Big Cheese* because of its yellow paint scheme was a behemoth piece of engineering. When buckled in his seat, he was perched some twenty five feet up. The push blade measured seventy two feet long and sixteen feet high. Behind the blade was a series of large wire brushes that would sweep forward the smaller debris as he pushed. His focal points were a series of red and green lights on the far side of the barge. Being perched so high up, he could never discern his position so when a green light lit, he would push straight towards it until his tether stopped him and pulled him back up. He always said he liked it that way, not being able to see what and sometimes who he was sweeping and at the end of the day he could boast *"I'm not involved,"* and be perfectly fine with it.

"Hey what's up Frank?" Shooster asked in a cheerful voice.

"Mr. Shooster, garbage sweep extraordinaire, how are you my friend?"

"Doing just great, about another hour on this tractor and I can button this lid and head for the lounge for a well-deserved break."

Shooster paused, then it dawned on him, "I suppose you brought some personal cargo with you today?" he asked with a little chuckle.

"You know me all too well my good man. How about you take an early break and I'll tend to my business and finish your sweep for you?"

Shooster shut down the electric motor and dropped the big sweep blade on the deck, climbed off the tractor, walked over to the big glass window, held a hand up to indicate the OK sign and hurried off into the building.

Waste or garbage known as personal cargo was a fringe benefit of working on the barges. Unwritten rule is, no one ever asked what your personal cargo is and no one really cared. Many times crew members would make a little extra cash or credits by disposing of an illegal item or two. It was also common place to have friends or family on the sweeps dock to help you unload and dispose of your personal cargo. This way no one would ever question Frank and Kester when they struggled with the awkward bulky package that contained Porter's body. Frank and Kester muscled the cargo right to the end of the deck and dropped it on the wide yellow caution line. Kester put his hands on the small of his back standing up, he arched his back like he had just worked a full day of hard labor. This was the last thing Kester would remember doing on Earth. Frank scanned the sweeps area to see if Shooster remembered to hit the off switch on the security cameras. He did. Frank then walked over to the tractor and removed the metal rod from its round tube slot next to the left drive tread. The rod was used to stun any animals that might wander in or be dropped off for disposal. It carried ten thousand volts of electricity and it was said, but never tested, that it could drop a full grown elephant in a fraction of a second. Taking a second glance to see no one was around he walked up behind Kester, placed the rod in the center of his chest and pulsed enough electrical current through him to drop him on the spot. Frank Lewis quickly clambered aboard the tractor and pushed both Kester Trewer and Porters bodies off the sweeps deck and in to the barge before sweeping the rest of the waste on the deck on top of them. He tossed what was left of the dope on top of Kester's lifeless body.

With the deck clean and the tractor parked, Frank called for a button. Slowly a five inch thick composite plate was lowered on to the top of the barge. Robotic drills started splattering sparks in every direction for about an hour until the barge was permanently sealed. Eventually the massive ship would implode and then vaporize in the sun, that would be months from now. Frank figured Kester would be frozen to death in under an hour and if he was lucky he would stay unconscious until then.

It looked like Frank was the last of his crew left on Earth, all the others must have copped a ride in style or at least more style than his ride will be.

He stopped in the office and then took a quick look in the lounge. He found no one he was looking for, with a shrug of his shoulders he grabbed a handful of mints from the counter, ducked into the john to take a leak then headed towards the small but adequate three man cockpit placed at the front of the barge. He grabbed the rungs of the ladder which reached upward a good twenty five feet then took one final look before he ascended. The thick glass that was molded into a re enforced composite frame reflected the image of a man who looked like he needed a week's sleep. Frank punched in his security code, a wisp of oxygen escaped and he could feel the heat from inside. He placed his left foot up then swung his right around and dropped it onto the floor of the cockpit. Spinning on the ball of his foot he plopped down and pushed the button to close the glass shroud over his head. The seats were old and worn but still had some comfort left in them. He looked straight ahead, the rails seemed like a never ending strong line in front of him. He opened the communications channel then placed an ear bud securely in his ear.

"This is Frank Lewis in the barge Omega counting down and checking off." His voice transported to somewhere outside his imagination.

"Copy that Frank Lewis," a soft woman's voice returned.

"Is this my sweet lady Rosemary?" He asked with a slight rise in the pitch of his voice.

"The one and only Frank baby, you didn't think I would let you go without saying goodbye did you?"

"Oh darlin you sure no how to raise a man's blood pressure." He flirted back at her.

"Oxygen seal," she demanded.

"Check," he answered.

"Cabin pressure?"

"Check."

"Temperature?"

"Check again darlin."

"Emergency oxygen?"

"Check."

"G-force wrap in place?" G-force wraps were used to literally hold you together once you reached a certain speed. With low cabin pressure and no G-force wrap by the time you were launched you would have been unconscious if you were lucky. The wrap started at your feet and wrapped around your entire body like a boa constrictor. The faster the speed the tighter the wrap.

"Check darlin, the only thing missing now is you. What say I take you on the journey of a lifetime? Just me and you and the empty space. Floating around til the cows come home."

Rosemary laughed. "Til the cows come home?" She asked through the giggles. "You been watching those old movies again?"

"Awe come on Rose, don't be like that, a man gets pretty lonesome in space without a sweet lady."

In her most sexy voice Rose came back through his ear piece. "Last item on your check list hot stuff. You have what's left of your brains secure in your helmet?"

"Check, check and double check." Frank answered back with a thumbs up even though he knew Rosemary couldn't see it.

Without giving Frank time to blink, a trail of parallel green lights lit the path in front of him as far as he could see. Last thing Frank heard on Earth was Rosemary Turners voice wishing him God speed and a safe trip.

The G-force wrap tightened around Frank, the barge quietly lifted six inches from the ground and started to pace forward. Before he knew it, he was traveling somewhere in the vicinity of twenty six thousand miles per hour. The green lights turned into a solid green streak as he was held tight in his seat, everything was a blur for the next two minutes until he found himself lobbed out of Earth's atmosphere and into an orbit to align Barge Omega with Quincy 4 for its final journey.

The barge docked flawlessly next to Quincy 4. Frank exited through the air lock and made his way in to find the rest of the crew.

Departure

The crew was sitting in the lounge drinking coffee while waiting for final instructions. This was Quincy 4's last trip. She was a grand old ship, the last of its kind. Built on Earth and assembled in space. The sendoff was to be covered globally by the media as well as factory reps and interested citizens. Although there was debate about the fate of the tug, money ruled in the end as it usually does. Some wanted her docked at C-Gate 5 as a memorial. Some wanted her returned to port and turned into a museum, however the final decision, sad as it was, was to send her into the sun with her last load of waste. To be vaporized. Her fate was now set in ink. Each C-Gate she stopped at some of her vital internal components were scheduled to be removed. Computers, although years obsolete, security codes, mother boards, guidance and tracking systems will all be removed, leaving a mere shell of the grand ship she used to be to tack her way into history.

Her final stop at C-Gate 6 will find her being celebrated by the crew on board as well as twenty five other men and women who will then be out of a job. When C-Gate 6 closes with the passing of Quincy 4, all trajectories will be set on a new guidance path from C-Gate 5 thus rendering C-Gate 6 the furthest out derelict known to mankind. Eventually C-Gate 6 will drift into the Sun's gravitational pull and be vaporized. This however will not take place for hundreds of years if not thousands. The space travel conglomerates will have Jim Houtt install the solar power pack to the redundant life detection system already in operation. This system is designed to close the gate and return any vessel detecting life back to C-Gate 5. The physical gate itself holds a squad of twenty five men and women whose job it is to scan and detect any vessels that far out in space. The actual area in space known as C-Gate 6 is as vast as the radar scan can detect. With the modern laser radar technology that would be approximately one hundred and twenty five thousand mile radius before reception would be compromised.

A rep from The Three Day Shuttle Company walked into the lounge followed by a stewardess wheeling a cart of food and drinks. Also on the cart were several envelopes which she handed out to each of the crew members.

"Gentleman," the Rep said. "You will find your bonus in these envelopes along with a set of individual specific instructions. These instructions will be carried out to a tee in accordance to the amount of the bonus you've received."

In a tacky display of bad manners he picked up a handful of finger food and started to munch while he finished his speech.

"In a moment we will be visited by several dignitaries and heads of state from the entire planet including our own Governor Trewer. They're on their way to the global summit on C-gate 2. Last minute decision has them stopping here at Gate 1 for a photo op. He tossed some green thing in his mouth that looked inedible and continued.

"This meeting will be brief. This is a political meet and greet only. Answer their questions with as many yes and no answers as possible and please gentlemen..." He pause to get their full attention. "Please give them only need to know information and right now, and… they need to know nothing." The red haired stewardess was standing in the rear of the room next to the bar. Her hair was done up in a massive bee hive hairdo and her skin tight one piece jump suit was a welcome distraction to the men. He nodded to her, she then walked around the room handing out the bonus envelopes and offering them something to eat.

After hearing Governor Trewer was here. Frank, thinking, *"this is getting bigger than it needs to be,"* excused himself to the lavatory where he started to vomit. A cold disbelieve washed over him. His breathing became shallow and irregular. He started to panic. *"What were the odds of the Governor and his freshly dead son ending up at the same place at the same time?"*

"Hold on Frank," he said out loud. "Keep your head on."

Franks history with Governor Trewer and the fact Kester was sealed in the barge put him on the edge of some surreal mental trip. It was Trewer who sent him up to work the tracks for four years just to keep him quiet, and knowing the Governor and the Prime Minister of Canada were both responsible for the extra bodies found that day, he started to vomit again.

Just then the Rep whose name is Randolph walked in. Randolph knew most of the story between Governor Trewer and Frank.

"Please Boss, will you excuse me from this meeting?" Frank almost begging, wiped his mouth with a paper towel.

"I left lounge 3 unlocked you can wait for us in there," Randolph said then added with a stern tone in his voice. "Just make sure you find your way back when this fiasco is over...got it?"

"Yes sir and thank you." Frank answered as he headed towards lounge 3. Frank was no stranger to lounge 3. Lounge 3 was a holding tank for those returning from space that may or may not be carrying something illegal or banned on Earth. The dim lighting, cracked and peeling paint on the walls were never noticed as he ran to the bathroom to vomit again. Looking at his face in the mirror, splashing water on it he asked himself out loud, "what are the chances?"

William arrived back to 4335 West Polk Rd after dropping Governor Trewer off. He was about to enter his security code to open the front gate when a craving hit. He figured by now Kester would be too stoned, drunk or both and out of commission until morning so he turned the limo around and headed back to town for a little self-indulgence. Fu Yong a small mom and pop restaurant specialized in all foods eastern. He liked the shark fin soup and spicy wrapped beef with just enough sake to take the edge off. He pulled off the exit and drove the four miles to the restaurant parked his car and walked in. He was greeted by a small thin man with shiny black hair that was never combed but always clean.

"Good evening William," the man said.

"Evening," William returned the greeting with an outstretched hand. The proprietor took his hand and shook it.

"The usual tonight?" Max asked.

"You know it," William answered following a young attractive Chinese woman to a secluded booth. Max; born Xjnxg Gow Cho in a small village about three hundred miles south of Beijing China gave up years ago trying to teach Americans how to pronounce his name. Now he tells anyone who has the courtesy to ask, to just call him Max. Fifteen minutes later William was savoring the brilliant flavors placed before him. He figured the Governor was resting quietly in his berth, Kester was stoned somewhere on the grounds or in the house and everything was just peachy in his little world....he figured wrong.

Content but feeling alone, William headed back home. He took the long way driving through China Town. The sights, the smells and the people created a dream like state. He knew where he could find some paid for company along with the well-hidden opium dens. He also knew if he continued to romance those thoughts it could be days before he ever left China Town if he didn't leave now.

Entering the service road at the back of the estate he punched in his security code and sat there waiting as the back gate screeched open. Thinking he really needs to have that thing adjusted and lubricated soon. He pulled through and waited for the gate to clang shut behind him. Parking in the five car garage he immediately noticed the empty spot. Kester better not get pulled over by the cops, he thought then secondly thinking what a foolish thought the first thought was. No cop in his right mind would pull over that spoiled excuse of a man, if he or she knew what was good for them. William parked his car, walked out of the garage past the herb garden leading to the pool and stopped in his tracks. Blood was everywhere and from where he was standing his mind raced and his heart sank. He knew this day would come but none the less he was still taken by surprise. Cautiously he walked closer, not wanting to disturb the scene. Expecting to find a body, there was none. However what he did see almost caused his expensive dinner to come up. Blood and human tissue which he was almost sure were brains splattered all over the glass doors leading to the house. He knew he had to collect his thoughts before he made any calls.

Chapter 2

(The deal)

Space became the big prostitute of the twenty third century. If it wasn't worth anything or needed to be removed from Earth...space was the answer. Enough money, lives and time were thrown into construction and maintenance of the rails worldwide, everyone conceded to the reality they were here to stay. However, pointless protests and political bantering was it remained a topic just about daily. Many political platforms were won and lost on the subject of space dumping. The biggest problem concerning the rails was the amount of land required to construct and operate them. North America alone grabbed up hundreds of thousands of square miles of land to use for the operations and maintenance purposes. A strict parameter of ten miles on each side of a rail was established early on. This meant if you had a rail that was twenty miles long, it ran straight through four hundred square miles of unusable property. Property which was taken from its owners, sometimes by deadly force.

After the failed North American summit of 2232, the world's leaders agreed upon retreating the designated rail parameters from ten miles to two miles. This was referred to as the mass land grab of the twenty third century. Rail towns boomed overnight. The economic success was a surprise to everyone who was lucky enough and had the foresight enough to realize the financial potential of a new town. This did however put a new spin on the old term *"the other side of the tracks"*. Forbidden not only by law but also by physics and safety, you could not go over or under the rail for any reason. The law stated anyone caught inside the two mile parameter was immediately arrested and automatically placed on a hard labor schedule working on the rail for not less than four years, with no trial and no questions.

Five years earlier

Governor Trewer sat down on the cold steel framed chair inside the interrogation room. The room itself was cold and empty. One table and three chairs. The table had a metal ring welded to it for running a chain through to secure the prisoner. He had asked for room number five for a specific reason and that being there was no two way mirror or microphones installed in that room. Interrogation room five was the one room nobody wanted to visit. More times than not a prisoner would leave covered up dead.

The governor's heart jumped out of his chest with a startle when the big door clicked as it was unlocked. He jerked his head around with every intention of telling the guard how startled he was. Instead Frank Lewis was lead in first and Trewer was by no means going to allow Frank to see that as a weakness.

"Good morning Governor," the guard said as he plopped Frank down and cuffed him to the metal hoop on the table.

"I see you picked room number five," He then leaned in and whispered into Frank's ear. "Not sure what you did Francis but this is the room nobody leaves alive." He placed his hand on Frank's cheek and slightly slapped him in mock affection.

Sweat broke out on Frank's face and he couldn't manage to utter a sound. All he could do was look at Roman Trewer and wonder, had he somehow missed something in his calculation. The guard walked to the door making sure he stayed in the eyesight of both men. He stopped and waited for them to look his way. Pulling a night stick from his holster and laying it on the floor next to the door, rolled up his pant leg and produced a small caliber pistol. He held it up, winked at Frank and said to The Governor. "This one is my back up, can't be traced and no one will have access to this wing of the jail until nine o'clock tomorrow morning. All the doors will automatically lock behind you on your way out." He walked out.

Governor Trewer picked up the night stick and slammed it down on Frank's hand. Frank tried to hold back his scream which only resulted in him spitting and blowing snot all over himself. He looked at Trewer with angry pain in his eyes but said nothing. This time the stick was placed under his chin lifting his eyes up to meet the Governor's.

"So" said Governor Trewer. "You know something that I don't." He eased the pressure a little bit.

Frank still trying to digest the fact he was never going to be in control of this situation started searching his mind for the right thing to say. Trewer raised the night stick.

"Ok, ok" Frank said, slobbering spit down the front of his orange prison jump suit. "How was I sposed to know?" He blurted out.

"Know? Know what Frank?"

"How was I sposed to know that your doper punk son was setting you up? For some messed up reason I thought you were in on it too."

"Hold on a minute." Trewer said just as the night stick came down again on Frank's hand. This time Frank puffed his cheeks up and blew out a foul smell of air between his grinding teeth.

"Please stop that, Roman." He managed to say.

"You thought I was in on this? Whatever gave you the idea I was in on this?" He looked at Frank's hands which were now starting to turn purple across the tops.

Frank was trying to move his fingers and wincing at every bend of a knuckle. "Didn't you have the security and guns shut down so we could get to the rail?" Looking at Governor Trewer with a puzzled look on his face.

"I did no such thing Frank," he answered turning his back on him, he walked over and picked up the pistol.

"Hey man!" Frank was shaking his head back and forth. "You going to shoot me now?" Panic was setting in on Frank Lewis.

Governor Trewer placed the gun against Frank's head and said, "tell me why I shouldn't." He pulled the trigger in slightly. "You know how many of your idiots were killed. And it wasn't six … was it? And if I let you walk out of here my career is over."

"Yeah, well let me tell you this much man, if I have to take the rap for those four and your two, you might as well just shoot me now anyhow. I'll never see the light of day again" Frank was feeling more stupid and angry with himself by the minute. He never expected Trewer to stand up to him like this. He figured from the start he had the upper hand.

"You realize if I let you live, the guards will figure you have some dirt on me right?" Trewer said as he jammed the cold barrel of the gun against Frank's head.

"Man you can't just kill me, not like this. I mean, look at all the times I saved that son of yours from himself. You know he'd be dead by now five times over if it were not for me." His fingers were now curled into themselves like a man with severe arthritis.

"I personally would not be in this spot if he were dead, so don't mistake your duties for kindness because they were a necessity. You were paid well and I owe you nothing." He pulled the trigger to the pistol. Frank jumped from his chair until the length of chain pulled him back forward. He let out a squeal like a little girl and messed himself as the gun clicked to the sound of an empty chamber. Trewer then picked up the nightstick again, and beat Frank about the face and head until he was nearly unrecognizable.

"I'll be back in two days, if you're still alive when I return we'll discuss the terms of your sentence." He made a sniffing motion to the air and said, "And clean yourself up you smell like crap."

The slam of the cold cell door was inaudible through his ringing ears. Frank had been beaten many times before, he knew he would recover but it was going to take a long time. He also wondered why he was left to live instead of left to die.

Just after midnight, sitting in his study drinking himself into another fear driven stupor, Prime Minster Wells picked up his secure line to call Governor Trewer.

"Hello?" The governor answered his phone.
"Roman this is Barry, and I need to know you have everything under control and cleaned up."

"I know who you are you drunken idiot, you called me on our secure line and I refuse to discuss this issue with you until you're in better shape!" He slammed the phone down and left a voice message for his secretary to arrange a military rail with top priority for first thing in the morning. Destination Prime Minister Barry Wells of Canada.

The following morning the two men sat across from one another at a small oak table just off the Prime Minister's private kitchen. Governor Trewer was nursing a cup of real coffee and Prime Minister Wells was nursing a hangover.

"His name is Frank, and that's all you need to know." Trewer told the Prime Minister.

"He was caught inside the parameter and hauled off just minutes before the disaster. We can't pin the sabotage on him or the dead bodies since the brilliant security officer already had him five miles from the scene, but he still believes we can still pin it on him."

"What about the press leak?" Wells asked

"Nothing more we can do about it now. Our press secretary recanted the leak as best we could and people will forget. They always forget." turning his face away from Wells.
"Excuse me Roman!" Wells said as his voice began to get louder. "You expect me to believe in the light of the only disaster on the rails since its inception that it will be forgotten?" His head felt like it was about to explode. "We have dead people there, Roman, dead people! Dead people you and I are responsible for!"

"Not just you and I Barry, Frank too. Frank is responsible for dead bodies inside the rail too. All we have to do is get him to confess and then.... I guess he'll accidentally fall down a flight of stairs too."

Prime Minister Wells stopped sipping his Bloody Mary, looked over the edge of his glass. "You didn't?"

"Of course I did, are you kidding me? Our press secretary was the only person to have seen with his own eyes the remains of six people and Frank is the only other person besides us who knows it. And as far as the public will ever know, it was just sabotage on the rail and no loss of life will ever be mentioned again." He sipped his coffee. "And look at it this way, your blackmailers are gone, your country is spared, your family is spared the embarrassment of a scandal and our lives go on like it never happened."

Prime Minister Wells never turned around to face Governor Trewer "He lives." Wells said in a soft tone. "This Frank you have in lock up... he stays alive."

Governor Trewer tried to speak but Wells just waved a hand behind his back to shut him up.

"I'm telling you, he stays alive. That's my insurance policy and if you think for one moment, I'm going to trust you to be quiet you've made a serious miscalculation Roman. As long as Frank is alive and facing life at hard labor on the rails, we're both safe. And so help me Roman, if he accidentally falls down a flight of stairs I will accidentally leak the names of the activists you hire to keep heat on your political advances. The way I see it, we have three men who all depend on each other to remain quiet. Now please leave my office and my home."

Governor Roman Trewer sat his coffee cup down gently on the table, wiped his lips with a napkin and said, "why Barry, I'm crushed you don't trust me, I thought we were friends. Besides I need to find me a new press secretary, preferably one that can keep his mouth shut," and walked out.

"Frank!" The guard said "Wake up man, Governor Trewer is here with your sentence."

Slowly and painfully Frank opened the one eye that was not swollen shut. He tried to talk but his words just came out like a jumbled mass of gurgles and wincing moans.

"Relax Frank, just lay there, I'll read you your sentence. The guard will witness it and I'll give you thirty days to heal before we put you on the rail."

"Francis Bain Lewis on this day, 16 of September 2237 you have been convicted of trespassing on government owned property. This carries a mandatory sentence of not less than four years of hard labor on the rail. You will remain here in County lock down in the medical ward until 15 October 2237 at which time you will be transported by military rail to an undisclosed location where you begin to serve your term as Yoman on the rail for the minimum sentence of four years. You will be released from

Government custody on 16 September 2241. If your time on the rail is served without any trouble you will able to retain your position as an employee of the United Rail Systems." This Frank already knew, being part of the negotiation team to have constructed the language in the last contract. His job was safe as long as he was alive. Governor Trewer turned, walked out of the cell and hoped he would never see Francis (Yoman) Bain Lewis again.

Yoman – The position

The position of Yoman on the rails was specific to leniency. Many times Yomen were looked upon as those who received a mandatory sentence with extenuating circumstances. For instance some kid got drunk and managed to find his way in the illegal parameters of the track, the sentence of Yoman would be appropriate. Many of the female violators who were not political prisoners were giving the choice between Yoman or Domestic Counsel. Domestic counsel was just as it sounded. With hundreds of thousands of workers daily, needing to be fed and cared for The Domestic Counsel handled all those needs and a few other desires for the workers if the price was right.

The Job of the Yoman was to see that materials and tools were where they needed to be at all times. A high stress position and very rarely one of a physical nature The Yoman was looked down on from everyone else who was sentenced to hard labor. It was not uncommon to find a dead Yoman stuffed under a concrete slab from time to time or just come up missing. Once given the title of Yoman this became your identity for the duration of your sentence and for many, the rest of their lives.

Chapter 3

(The last summit held on Earth)

The lights of the board room were dim, as the early morning rays cast their first sign of the sunny day forecast for September 12, 2232.

Today's United World conference was not going to be an easy one. The caterers neatly arranged place settings at each chair. Started the coffee brewing and eloquently arranged a colorful assortment of breakfast rolls and fruit on five large platters. They then spaced them perfectly on the gigantic oak table. In about half an hour from now at eight o'clock, all the heads of state of the countries who represent, what society was now calling *"space dumping,"* would soon be seated for what was looking to be an extremely long day. Satisfied with the way the table looked, the head hostess, a very pretty thin brunette named Dawn, announced to the rest of her staff to meet in the kitchen immediately.

"Ok ladies," she said, as she reached in a pink and purple decorated box for a breakfast roll. She pulled out one with bright yellow frosting then passed the box. "Remember we see nothing and we hear nothing. No matter what your personal or political views are on space dumping. The board room and its delegates are one hundred percent off limits."

She took a bite, poured herself a cup of coffee and nodded to her staff to enjoy the extra food.

Security guards showed up and started to walk through the kitchen. Each guard carried an automatic machine gun on their shoulder as well as a stun gun, baton and a pair of handcuffs on their belt. As they filtered in, their conversation turned to commenting on the smell of the coffee and the several boxes of left over fruit and breakfast rolls.

By the time Dawn figured out the guards discretely positioned themselves at all three exits and surrounded the rest of the hostesses, it was too late to act. Another man walked in. He was wearing a dark blue suit with a red pin stripped tie and carrying a clipboard.

"How can I help you?" Dawn asked the man carrying the clipboard.

He looked up, without saying a word he walked past the hostesses who were now lined up like they were in line for an inspection.

"This one," he said pointing to a slightly heavy set woman with her hair tied up.

Immediately an armed guard approached the woman and stood in front of her pointing his gun directly at her mid-section.

"Now hold up a minute here!" Dawn bellowed at the man.

He turned and approached her. With a steel gray stare in his eyes he reached into his blazer pocket and produced a small but very effective high voltage zapper, oddly enough sold anywhere on any street corner by the name "The Zapper." His gaze never wavered from Dawn's eyes, he placed the zapper against her stomach and pushed a small button where a trigger on a standard fire arm would be, Dawn dropped to the floor and lay there twitching and jerking in her own urine.

"She'll be fine in about an hour." The suited man said as he continued to size up the rest of the hostesses. He stopped in front of another lady. "This one too," he said as the woman started to visibly shake and sweat.

Two more steps and he stopped again. "This is the last one up here," he said while standing in front of an extremely attractive Asian woman. He placed his hand under her chin and lifted her face so she could look into his eyes.

"Pity too, this one is a real looker."

She furrowed her eyebrows and then spit in his face.

"I'll deal with you personally outside," he told her with a smile on his face. He picked up a napkin and wiped her spit from his face.

He grabbed a breakfast roll, stuck it in his mouth, bit off a piece then said, "let's get these three out of here, we have an entire floor to search." The three ladies were escorted out each wearing handcuffs and none of them saying a word.

The man in the suit walked over to Dawn who was now sitting up. He reached out his hand to help her up. She laughed at the gesture and stood on her own.

"I would apologize ma'am but that's not my job. My job is to see this debate and summit goes on without a disruption of any kind and the three we just pulled out of here were on my list of top ten terrorists." He suggested Dawn take a shower, change her clothes and meet him in the board room in fifteen minutes. As a humorous touch to his demand he placed his hand on his zapper and smiled. He then dismissed the rest of her staff, walked in and sat down at the head of the board table and waited.

Angry mobs converged in the square outside the building. Some carrying signs reading, "No more space dump." Some were climbing the flag poles and removing the flags representing the countries at the summit. Some were climbing fences and shaking a defiant fist in the air and all were inside the five hundred foot parameter the police had set up. The masses were protesting about hundreds of thousands of square miles of land owned by the government and businesses just sitting there empty. And their biggest concern was the Earth's garbage being returned from the sun in the form of deadly radiation. It was no secret to anyone about the nuclear and biological waste the military disposed of by way of space dumping. And some were there simply because they had no place else to be.

There was no scientific proof to confirm deadly radiation was returning to Earth. Many scientist throughout the world who were studying the cause and affects could not be pinned down to give an answer. However there was plenty of speculation and conspiracy theories to fuel the unrest and threat of uprisings that the world leaders decided to at least sit down and discuss the issues.

Fifteen miles out the red and green lights on the military rail lit up. Four hundred military men and woman armed with riot gear boarded several tram cars and headed into town. They were silently railed in through the service entrances located in sub level 3 of the building. The same service level the heads of state, dignitaries and delegates would enter from, in less than an hour. Within minutes they started to congregate in the basement of The United World building. Once all four hundred were inside they quickly reached the ground level and started to show their presence. It took a good minute before the crowd outside noticed them, and the potential for some serious head bashing.

Dawn finished with her shower, donned a clean uniform and made her way back to the board room. The man who zapped her stood up when she walked in and acted like nothing had happened.

"Hi," he said tapping his badge. "I'm Sergeant Detective Martin Smith with the World Security Bureau department of foreign and domestic protection."

Dawn ignored the fact he wanted to shake her hand and started to pull out a chair to sit down.

"Here let me get that for you." Martin said reaching for the chair.

"Thanks but no," Dawn retorted "You have done enough for me for one day."

The detective still offered no apology. He sat back down and opened his brief case.

He tossed a manila folder on the table in front of Dawn, she opened it to take a look. Inside was a complete dossier on the first woman he approached in her kitchen. Dawn scanned through it.

She glanced up. "Are you kidding me?" She asked. "This woman's real name is Martha Washington?"

"Yeah I know, the irony of life, right?" Martin replied "Please read on Ms. Richards."

Dawn glanced up at the sound of her last name being mentioned knowing she never gave it to the man but then figured it was his job to know these things. She skimmed through the file, taking some extra time to study a few pictures that were taken in her kitchen.

"You guys hid cameras in my kitchen?"

"Relax Miss Richards, there's nothing on those cameras that will get back to your owner, but I'm glad to see I'm not the only person around who likes cheese cake after a nice healthy steak."

She brushed him off with a wave of her hand. "We're allowed to eat what's not served to our guests." She looked up at Martin. "I have known Sue for almost three years now, or should I call her Martha?"

Martin reached in front of her, reopened the folder, flipped a few pages, placed his forefinger on a list of names then said. "You can call her by anyone of these six aliases."

He slid another dossier over to her. She glanced up at him while opening the folder.

"May Li Ping?" She asked.

Martin nodded.

"She told me her name was Mary Ellen Pride from Wisconsin."

"May Ping was smuggled into the states about seven months ago from China. She is a ruthless killer and cold as ice. No doubt you would have met your maker today had we not shown up. But you can relax Ms. Richards, we had agents in the building for the last ninety days. You and your staff have been in good hands since."

Dawn mumbled under her breath a few choice words regarding her being zapped and started to look physically shaken up.

The third and final dossier was presented to her. She opened it up and was not disappointed to find the third woman also went by several names. She was however surprised to read she was from this town. She called herself Sara in her kitchen but her birth name was, of all things was Mildred.

Dawn thought *"I would have several aliases too if my name were Mildred."* So what are you going to do with them?" She asked.

"Mildred and Martha are both U.S. citizens and will be tried in Political Court. My guess would be they will be put to death. May Ping on the other hand, a Chinese woman sent here to assassinate dignitaries and delegates. China won't even admit she's here let alone take her back and according to the power given to me by the World Security Bureau I get the dubious honors of terminating her life, which will take place sometime tomorrow morning." He closed the folders then added. "Wanna watch?"

Dawn jerked her head up with the look of horrific surprise. "I'm good on that one but thanks for asking. ... Are we done here now?"

"One more thing." Martin said. He held his lapel close to his mouth and spoke into a little microphone. "Ok bring in the food."

The doors to the conference room burst open and a flurry of activity took place as a dozen smartly dressed women paraded in with a new batch of breakfast rolls and fresh fruit, followed by three men dressed in hazmat suits. Each carrying a steel container with a vacuum sealer attached to each lid.

Once again Dawn looked horrified.

"Did you or anyone on your staff eat from any of these trays Ms. Richards?"

"No, I didn't but I can only speak for myself. I don't think any of my girls would, I mean we get all the food we can eat in the kitchen and we have a strict policy about the food placed in the conference rooms, why?"

"Well, apparently Paula Fairchild did, because they found her foaming from her mouth dead in sub level 2. She was the victim of a poisoned breakfast roll. I'm sorry."

He held up a small spray bottle half full with a clear fluid. It was labeled with a mouthwash logo on the outside.

"This is what May Li used to poison the rolls after you placed them on the table. We have no clue yet, as to what type of poison she used. All we know is, she brought it from China and she spritzed all the trays of fruit and rolls with it.

Dawn stood up. "I think I'm gonna throw up now. Please excuse me." She started to leave when Martin spoke up again.

"Ms. Richards I cannot allow you to leave this building, nor can I allow you to be alone. I have assigned Officer Kelly Danson to accompany you for the next three days. You'll be staying with us here in the building in one of the suites upstairs as our guest. Anything you need or want until you leave is on us, so please I encourage you to indulge and enjoy your stay as best you can."

Dawn rolled her eyes and shot daggers at Martin, turned and huffed out the door, followed by Officer Kelly Danson.

Launch Rail #14

(East side 10:23 a.m.)

"It's perfectly safe." Frank Lewis told the other four men who had managed to tunnel their way into a secure area of Rail #14. "I got people on the inside. The scanners and the auto guns have been turned off from the outside. We have thirteen minutes to place these charges and get out."

They were all dressed in maintenance uniforms just in case. The smallest of the four men lugged a leather bag through the crude hole dug under the fence. He baulked when he finally reached the twenty foot high concrete barrier of the rail.

"You got to be kidding me?" He quipped. "You expect us to scale this wall?"

One of the other men just pushed him aside. Without saying a word he pushed the grappling hook into the spring loaded delivery system then fired the hook up over the wall. One at a time the four men scaled the wall where they rested on top to wait for Frank.

Frank poked his head out the hole, then hollered up. "Hey man I forgot the drill for the charges. You guys go in and I'll be right there."

Without giving their instructions a second thought the four men lowered themselves down into the rail area. They had never seen the rails from inside the concrete before. One long straight line for sixteen miles. They were standing next to a marking on the concrete wall that read mile nine which meant they were seven miles from the ocean and the launch apex.

"Hey man where's Frank?" One of the men asked.

"He'll be along he went back to get the drill so we can bore the holes for the charges."

"You mean this drill?" The first man said, holding up a fully charged cordless drill.

"Yeppers that would be the drill."

They started laughing.

"How stupid is Frank, he probably walked all the way back to the transport too."

"Yeah man, by the time he gets all the way there and back, we'll be finished." Said the small man who now had two of the eight holes bored.

"Here you go, I got two holes ready for charges."

The third man pulled out eight military explosive charges from the leather bag and laid them out on the ground.

After about eight minutes the job was complete. The charges were set and primed.

"No turning back now. In half an hour this rail will be history just in time for the eleven a.m. launch."

As the four men turned to climb back up the wall they all stopped in horrible awe at the fact there was no way for them to get back over the wall. Frank never joined them which meant the cable for the grappling hook was still on the outside of the wall.

"Leave it to Frank to cut this down to the wire getting us out of here." The tallest of the four men said.

On the outside of the wall, Frank was sitting next to a Rail Security transport vehicle in handcuffs. He was caught crawling back in to see that his partners in crime would have the cable to the grappling hook so they could get back over the wall.

He knew the law. Any civilian caught inside the fenced in area was an automatic four years hard labor on the rails and Frank was not about to tell the security there were four other men inside. It was now 10:53, there was no way they could be rescued in seven minutes. They hauled him away just about the same time the lights inside the concrete barrier turned on. Green and red alternating as far as the eye can see in both directions. The four men inside knew there was no hope for them now. Just then the magnets were charged, the steel grappling hook flung itself off the top of the wall in lightning speed and stuck fast to the closest magnet. Everything metal the four men had on them was either stripped or ripped from them and attracted to the nearest magnet also. They looked at each other in horror. Then they looked at the wall, still no cable. They looked at each other again when finally the smallest of the four men, now holding his pants up in his hands since the metal fasteners were ripped right off them, yelled "RUUUUUUUNNNNNN!" They started to run towards the ocean hoping that somehow they would survive if they managed to put some distance between them and the explosive charges. One by one, the men stopped running, out of breath and still miles from the apex. They were far enough away from the blast for it to not directly kill them when all the lights turned green. The tall man stood there watching the barge approach. He glanced over to the wall, the numbers on the white concrete wall indicated to him, he was now five and three quarter miles from the apex. He also noticed his three cohorts were lying flat on the ground. All he could do was stare at the monster barge heading towards him. Although this was by definition a smaller barge known as a piggy back, it still measured twenty five feet high, twenty five feet wide and sixty five feet long. Piggy back barges were connected by fours once in space before being tugged towards the sun. He could now feel a slight draft as the barge started to push the wind inside the concrete walls ahead of it. He stood there defiantly feeling the wind pick up, watching the barge grow with acceleration.

The first set of charges went off causing the barge to lift slightly. The second set of charges detonated causing the barge to severely shift to the left. It bounced in to the concrete wall, tearing out the electro magnets on that side of the wall. Those magnets began to flip and tumble next to the barge, bouncing and striking the barge alongside it. The third set of charges blew the barge back across to the other side, slamming it hard against the wall. This caused the barge to break open. White powder from the wall, electro magnets and debris from the barge headed towards the men. The fourth and final set of charges went off on both sides of the barge at the precise moment the barge reached them. This opened the front of the barge causing it to lift a good fifteen feet into the air and start to tumble, scattering pieces of itself and the debris inside like a shot gun full of buck shot. By the time the man standing could feel the heat from the explosions being pushed in front of the barge, his three friends were already dismembered and collected up in the debris field fast approaching. A fraction of a second later, what was left of his clothing was blown completely off and he became several more pieces of out of control tumbling debris. A barge traveling at that speed carrying that much weight bouncing off the concrete wall, ripping the large magnets from the rail system and strewing garbage and debris for three and a half miles. The rail was completely destroyed and beyond repair.

Meanwhile across town

The debate started at 11 a.m. right on schedule that day. Governor Roman Trewer in his opening statement made it clear that it was not the intentions of The United States and Canada's government to see the rails shut down. However, he contended it was the voice of many of their citizens and judging by the events not only in North America but now worldwide, there would have to be some kind of conclusion reached soon to pacify the masses. He shared with the representatives from around the world, his biggest fear would be all out civil warfare on a global scale.

China stood up and called North America weak and afraid to handle the situation with force. Citing the squash of civil unrest there due to a strong police force with no reservations to use any force necessary to control its people, up to, and including death.

The governor assured those at the table that death on a scale that large was never going to be considered and that North America despite its new views on population unrest and discipline were more demanding than they'd ever been. However, they were not going to become a killing machine.

Prime Minister Barry Wells from Canada spoke up about the possibility of moving their rail system as far north as they could. But then again the cost of such a venture would require financial backing from every country present, including China. It was becoming clear that day one of the debate was starting out difficult. It was also becoming clear that if China pulled out, this would be the last day of the debates. Just then buzzers and beepers started going off in the entire conference room. Governor Trewer watched with puzzled amusement. Then his wry smile faded when all the dignitaries in the room were giving him a blank stare. He glanced over to Prime Minister Wells who could only nod towards Trewer's personal communicator sitting on the table in front of him with its red light blinking. With a sickening look on the Governor's face, he picked up his device and read the news blurb that was scrolling across its tiny screen.

At first he thought it was some protesters off color antics. Maybe the devices were hacked? He placed his finger on the intercom button and called for his secretary to join him in the conference room. This was met with strong objections from few of the other heads of state present, including China so Trewer met his secretary at the door.

"Is this real or a prank?" He asked her with tears in his eyes. He was hoping she would tell him it was, but knew deep in the pit of his gut it wasn't.

"I'm afraid sir this is the real thing." She lowered her eyes when she answered him. "Would you like me to contact anyone for you?"

"No not right now I have to figure out what I'm going to do with those over there." He moved his eyes in the direction of the conference table. "On second thought Anne, see if you can get the white house to designate an open line and I'll call them as soon as I can."

"Yes sir," she managed a smile. "This could have happened in any one of the countries here today just as easy." She turned to leave.

"Yeah it could have but it didn't."

Governor Trewer walked back to the cold steel gray stares of the most powerful men and women in the world, embarrassed, humiliated and angry. "Ladies and gentlemen as you already know, Rail #14 was sabotaged moments ago not only stopping the 11a.m. launch but it destroyed the entire rail system. At least that's the information we have received thus far."

He nodded towards the door and several young attractive men and women walked in. "Please try to understand our position here today and the need for complete compliance." He glanced around the table to see if he could tell if any of the guests were going to cause trouble. "I regret to inform you that a complete sequester is the standard emergency procedure and until we get an all clear I will have to ask each and every one of you to go back to your rooms and remain there." He had a hard time looking them in the face. "The World Security Bureau has provided each of you with your own personal page and no expense will be spared into looking after your comforts."

He packed up his briefcase and then added. "Now if you will excuse me, it seems I have a serious issue that requires my immediate attention."

Prime Minister Wells met the Governor at the door. Shook his hand and leaned in for what he hoped would look like a consolatory hug. "Please tell me our cargo was not on the barge?" He whispered.

"Now is not the time or the place to be thinking about that, let alone bring it up." Trewer whispered back.

He turned and bowed gracefully to those who present then exited the conference room. He approached his secretary Anne on his way out.

"Do you think you can handle this with me or should I request someone else?"

Anne was quick with her answer. "Yes sir. I'm your girl and to be honest I doubt I could keep my trap shut if you left me here. I would feel the need to defend you at least, if not the whole country."

They rode the elevator to sub level 3 where a transport was waiting. He punched in a code to override all the rails from here to the crash site. He called Detective Sargent Martin Smith for an emergency access code and in less than ten minutes he and Anne stepped off the tram to catch a ground coach to what remained of Rail #14.

Frank Lewis was now sitting in lock up with a blank stare on his face waiting for his attorney to show up.

"So Francis," the investigating officer said. "Looks like we got you for trespassing and vandalism for starters. You ever do hard labor Francis?" He smiled as the condescension rolled off his tongue.

Frank never looked up and refused to be taunted into uttering a single word. He knew his attorney would be there soon. He also knew who was behind turning off the scanners and the auto guns. That would be none other than Kester Trewer the junky son of the beloved governor himself. He was feeling pretty confident he was going to walk away from this, as long as he couldn't be connected to those dead bodies. Being in lock down he had no access to any media and that drove him crazy. His attorney showed up and within the hour Francis Bain Lewis was moved from the holding tank to his new cell. For the next four years there was nothing his attorney could do for him.

Governor Trewer and his secretary Anne rolled up to Rail #14 to find a circus of media and military aimlessly wandering around. There were no barricades set up, there was no security set up and there was no order. The scene on the outside of the rail was complete chaos.

"Are those media drones flying over the rail?" Anne asked.

"It appears to be that way," Trewer answered.

"Correct me if I'm wrong sir, but I thought all rails have imposed a no fly zone over head."

"Good point, except language of the law states all functioning rails and this rail is far from functional." He walked up to the first soldier he could find. "Who's in charge here?" He asked in a voice that demanded a quick response.

The soldier pointed to his commanding officer who was standing about a hundred yards away.

"That would be Captain Moss, Sir, the one with the bars on his shirt."

"I know what captains bars look like you idiot." He barked back to the soldier who now looked like a hurt puppy.

"Yes Sir! No disrespect intended Sir." His words fell on deaf ears as Trewer was already walking briskly towards the Captain.

Anne walked up to the soldier, he was a good looking young man of about twenty three. She placed a soft hand on his shoulder and said, "He's not upset with you I hope you know that." She smiled and walked away not even trying to catch her bosses pace.

Governor Trewer walked up to the officer. "Captain Moss?"

"Yes I am Captain Moss and you are?" He said with a light tone of patronization.

"I am Governor Roman Trewer and I beg you not to use that tone again during this conversation."

"Yes Sir, sorry Sir, how can I be of assistance to you Sir?"

Anne snickered and Trewer shot her glance.

"How about for starters, why have you not secured this parameter? I do believe protocol requires a complete media blackout and a parameter of no less than five hundred feet?"

"Yes sir I am aware of the law and the protocol; but...."

Trewer grabbed Moss by his elbow and walked him out of Anne's ear shot. "Listen to me and listen to me good, Captain" Trewer now had fire in his eyes. "This is my show and you will do as I say. I give you my word I'll take full responsibility for any fall out. But I need to tell you straight up, if you have any men inside that concrete barrier I will court martial the lot, and you my friend will face a firing squad...coppice? And just in case you don't know what that means... that's Italian for comprendia which is Spanish for, you picking up on what I'm putting down?

Captain Moss was burning with anger but he knew better than to challenge this situation. He despised moments like this in his military career when the chain of command was above him instead of below him.

"Now about these media drones." Trewer said pointing to the sky. There were seven news drones directly over the concrete barrier collecting data.

"Yes sir." Moss answered "But the law states…" and he was cut off by a firm finger poking him in his chest.

"With all due respect sir, please don't do that in front of my troops." Moss said while staring Trewer down.

The Governor removed his finger from Mosses chest but the stare down continued.

"I know what the law says about the no fly zone being unenforceable since this rail is now nonfunctional. I also know that the same law states any unauthorized persons or material on rail property are subject to seizure for a period of time not less than four years. "He then pointed up to the drones which now numbered eight and said. "If those drones were to crash, fall out of the sky, land or hmmmmm..." He placed a contemplative finger under his chin for a little sarcastic affect. Or...maybe be shot down, and just so happen to end up on rail property. I would say that solves our issue. Wouldn't you agree Captain?

"Sir?" Captain queried "You want me to give orders to shoot down the drones?"

"Between you and I, Captain, and this is on the record. I don't care how those drones find their way onto rail property. This is a matter of national security and once those planes are on rail property the news won't be allowed to use the footage they already have...so... make it happen Captain, by whatever force you deem necessary... and again just for the record. NO I am not ordering you to shoot down drones. I'm ordering you to take control.

Captain Moss gathered eight of his best sharp shooters and before Governor Trewer could have time to digest that conversation, the sky was empty and there eight piles of smoking wreckage on the ground and all eight piles were now property of the rails for no less than four years.

"Well now we'll see if The Beam still works," he said to Anne as the two of them sat down at a makeshift command center.

The Beam is a series of multi-color laser beams that criss cross along the exterior top of each rail system, virtually encasing the rail in a mixture of red, blue, green and yellow lasers to disrupt any view from above. Even though there is a no fly zone over each rail there is always the omnipresent satellites orbiting the Earth. The Beams are used on a daily basis for anything from personal privacy to national security on the private and military rail. The public transportation and launch rails never use them due to the high cost. Many of the beams stopped functioning years ago with the high cost of maintaining them

Governor Trewer called in a cleanup crew, which really presented a problem since this was the first time dealing with a mess like this. He was on the phone with Sgt. Smith discussing what he thought was needed.

"Ok Martin first let's try to activate The Beam," Trewer said.

"I'm sitting here at control panel A right now. I had anticipated your call," Smith said.

"Hit the switch and let's see what we have."

Sgt. Smith flipped up the black cover to reveal a green button and pushed it.

"All indicators on my panel acknowledge we have nothing, what's it look like on your end Roman?"

"Yeah we got nothing here too." Trewer answered. "I guess we do this the hard way. Ok Martin this is what we're going to need. We're going to need at least nine miles of cover. Something weather resistant and opaque. We're going to need a cleanup crew. I was thinking maybe your Men in White? Whatta ya think?"

Sgt. Smith paused before his answer. "Let me see what I have available and I'll get right back with you. In the meantime how about a maintenance crew to work on the beam?" Martin asked Trewer.

"I don't care as long as we treat this at the national security level it is."

Sgt. Smith did not quite get was Trewer was saying. He thought, *after all it's just nine miles of busted concrete, metal and garbage right? Where does that equate into a national security issue?*

Forty eight hours later the Governor's press secretary issued an official press release. Forty nine hours later he was accidentally tossed down a flight of stairs and pronounced dead at the scene.

As soon as the story broke about finding six dead bodies in the carnage of rail #14, Frank Lewis was moved to a solitary confinement cell. His new cell now measuring ten foot by ten foot. He started putting the puzzle pieces together in his mind and became quite proud of himself and with the finished results. He knew he was one of few people aware that there were two extra bodies found. This he was still hoping would work to his advantage because if it didn't his life was over. Frank was aware that the relationship between the Governor and his son Kester was one of distance and volatile at times. Kester became a financial drain on his father over the years with his drug addictions. Many times Kester would find himself behind on payments to loan sharks and drug dealers. It had been an unspoken desire of Kester to see his dad ruined or even dead, despite the fact he was the only man alive who ever helped him out. Now all he had to do was figure out who the other two bodies were and hope his scheme gets him out of prison.

Chapter 4

C-Gate 2 Present Day

William Moss stood just outside the blood splattered glass doors trying real hard not throw up his dinner.

Detective Brandon Miles was collecting evidence samples and barking out orders to the rest of the team in charge of the investigation. He was dressed in kakis with an unkempt blue button down shirt. William was not quite sure, but judging by the stain on the shirt it looked like Detective Miles had chili for lunch at least one day this week.

"Mr. Moss, let's go over your whereabouts one more time and then I'll have to ask you to come to the station to give a recorded statement."

"Yes sir," he answered with a tad of distain in his tone. "I left here exactly at 7:43."

"How do you know the exact time?"

"Because The Governor is a stickler about punctuality, 7:40 we were out the door. It took us three minutes to get to the garage and then to the gate. I always check my watch with the time in the Governors car. "He showed his watch to the detective. "This here is a genuine twentieth century top of the line time piece." The Rolex sparkled in the dim light.

"The Governors car is on atomic time but this here beauty has not lost one second of time since I've owned it.'" He raised the Rolex to his ear.

"Hey chief," one of his men called out. "We got some puke over here."

Puke meant DNA and this was exactly what the detective hoped they would find.

"Bag it up," he bellowed back at his man then returned his attention to his conversation. "Ok so it was 7:43 when you pulled out of here." He pointed at the watch with his pen before he scratched his head with it. "Then what?"

"We headed towards the launch terminal, we arrived precisely at 8:17."

The detective pointed at the watch again with his pencil.

"I dropped the Governor off and headed back here, I pulled up to the front gate at exactly 8:53."

Beating the detective to the punch, he held up his wrist to bring attention to the watch.

"So let me get this straight. You were gone one hour and ten minutes exactly. So all this took place in that short amount of time? And you didn't call it in until 10:27?" He finally looked up from his little blue note pad with a raised cyebrow.

"Not quite how the story goes" William said. I arrived back here at 8:53 then decided to drive back in to town for some dinner."

"Where did you go for your dinner?" Detective Miles interrupted

"Fu Young, a small mom and pop joint just this side of China Town." William answered with a touch of irritation now in his voice.

"And you can prove this?" The detective asked

"Yes I can, the owner and wait staff know me by name." He placed one leg up on the brick edge of the garden and started to bounce his knee.

"Nervous?"

"Nervous!" William raised his voice to the cop. "Are you kidding me? I got brains and blood all over this place, the governor's son is missing and you ask me if I'm nervous? Yea man! I'm a little nervous not to mention most likely out of a job too." He bent down, picked up a stone and tossed it across the garden.

"Please don't do that again Mr. Moss." Detective Miles instructed him. "This is a crime scene. Just one more question and you're good to go." He pulled the pencil from behind his ear and tapped the crystal of William's

Rolex with it. "Exactly what time did you arrive here to find the crime scene?"

"10:24," he flashed his watch in the direction of the detective.

William knew both gates on the property kept a record of all the times they open and closed including the duration of time spent opened. He also knew this was information he was not willingly going to surrender. "Are we finished now detective?"

"We are for now Mr. Moss, but I advise you not to leave this parish and you have twenty four hours to give me a recorded statement. Goodnight sir."

William started to walk towards the kitchen entrance when Detective Miles called out to him. "Crime scene Mr. Moss, can't stay here until our investigation is over. So sorry about that sir."

William shook his head, mumbled a few choice words under his breath, got back in the car and headed out the front gate. Looks like the prostitutes and opium dens in China town win. He turned left and headed back into town, lifting the Rolex to his ear again, and quietly laughed. "Stupid watch never kept correct time since I bought it." His tail lights disappeared in the night.

On Board Quincy 4

C-Gate 2

Jim Houtt the electrician or Sparky as some affectionately know him, was the first to settle into his command chair. A gray haired man in his mid-fifties, he had a pot belly from a diet of half eaten sandwiches which he always left lying around to eat the next day and enough coffee to keep Africa up all night. Sat comfortably reclined as his preflight check list scrolled in front of him in a light blue haze which reflected an eerie sheen off his glasses.

At his feet was perched a little personal foot locker. He slid a canvas bag in the locker and kicked it shut. It automatically locked. In the bag were two items he brought for this journey. A bottle of champagne to share with the flight crew just before Quincy 4 was sent on its final trajectory into the Sun and his personal journal. The journal contained a life time of wrong decisions, bad timing and failed relationships written in its pages. His intentions were to incinerate the journal and start fresh upon his return back home in approximately two years.

He reached out and flipped the toggle switch to open the main panel which contained all the controls he was responsible for. Every time he looked at his left hand it reminded him of his first trip on Quincy4 some thirty years ago and how he got the nick name of Sparky.
For a moment his mind wandered to that day when he really became acquainted with Quincy4
He was young, fresh out of electrical academy. His father pulled a few strings to get him aboard the ship and figured what better way for his son to become a man than sending him on a journey like this.
His first launch into space took him to shuttle base Kleopfer. Oddly named after Ron Kleopfer the man who owns the dubious title of the first man to retire from a labor position stationed on the moon.
Jim always thought that was a ridiculous honor but what did he know anyhow? Disembarked from the treadmill at the security station, he was standing in line to be searched when he was tapped on the shoulder. He turned his head to find a rather large woman whose name tag read Molly Reece smiling down at him.

"Mr. Houtt?" She inquired.

"Yes Ma'am," Houtt replied.

She gave him a scornful look. "Please call me Molly and follow me."

He wise cracked back to her, "you got it Molly, I'm following but can you tell me where and what this is all about?" She turned and smiled with a mouthful of perfectly straight white teeth "You *are* the new electrician correct?" Jim nodded and said, "in the flesh."

Molly disliked his freshness but she wasn't there to like the man. She was there to take him directly to the tug.
"Well" she said with an exasperated exhale pointing a stern finger at him. 'I believe we have an emergency which requires your expertise."

He thought he detected a little chuckle in her voice and felt a little nervous when he answered, "please lead the way."

She did. Molly walked him past all the security, down a brightly lit hallway and into a vast room with large plate glass windows.

The view from inside was awesome. He was looking out the huge windows at Quincy 4 the largest tug in service and the last to be built on Earth and assembled in zero gravity. She was truly a giant in size and dwarfed the modern more animated tugs of current.

Just then two men in red jumpsuits bearing the logo TTDSS which stood for The Three Day Shuttle Service walked in. "You Jim Houtt?" The shorter of the two asked. He smiled then reached his hand out to introduce himself. "I'm Mark Miland and this guy over here is Bob Stork. We been waiting for you."

Jim shook both men's hands then asked. "What seems to be the urgency here fellas?"

Follow us please and do was address as you Jim or Mr. Houtt?
Houtt smirked a little and said, "Jim is just fine."
Thinking, "*there sure is a lot of people following a lot of people around, around here.*"
The three of them entered the dock through an air lock then walked down a gang plank to a pair of steel doors. The door was lettered in big safety yellow letters Quincy 4.
The door opened and with a sweeping arm, Mark said, "Walk this way." Turned to his left. Houtt not missing an opportunity to be a wise crack swept his arm in an exaggerated motion and turned left as well.

With no time to soak in the awe of being in the presence of this giant ship Houtt found himself descending in an elevator down to sub level 3.
"Sub level 3." The automated voice in the elevator informed them of their arrival. The safety yellow letters on the door this time read *Ships Communications*.
Houtt had a feeling he was about to be tested and little he could do now to weasel his way out.
"We have a direct short circuit somewhere in our ships communications." Mark told him.
Bob interjected, "which means our computers are not talking to the ship." He turned and faced Jim. "Or the ship is not listening, take your pick."

Houtt was led to a work station complete with all the tools and manuals he would need. Bob and Mark turned to walk away when Mark pointed to the wall. "That black box over there on the wall is our intercom system.

Push the blue button for help. The red button is if you're in trouble. Good luck Chuck." The two men left the work station. When the vacuum seal on the door hissed then faded, for the first time in his life Jim Houtt really felt alone.

Baptism by fire, he thought, starting his visual inspection.
Circuit after circuit, mother board after mother board, all checked out.
  He was beginning to wonder if there really was a problem when he spotted a small scorched spot under the last mother board he just tested. Pulling a screw driver from his tool kit he removed the mother board then he removed the two screws that held the inspection panel cover.

  He smiled and said to himself, "dang I'm good, I mean, I'm really good."

  He pulled the circuit breaker, used his meter to check for current. Satisfied the circuit was dead he reached in to examine the wiring. He studied communication panels and mother boards extensively in the academy and he remembered his instructor telling the class about this particular situation. The mother board in question was a high/low voltage system very similar to the systems found in antiquated telephone circuits. The manufacturer had run the wrong gauge wire from the relay into the transformer so when the high voltage kicked in the wire gauge could not support the current and it subsequently fried itself.
He traced the wire back to its original connection and unplugged it. Piece of cake he thought. Replace the burned out circuit with a new one and rewire it with the proper gauge wire and then plug it in. How hard could this be? He rewired the new circuit and installed it. While he was plugging in the new circuit the rest of the crew was going over the final pre-launch steps. One of those steps included testing the redundant communication system. Houtt figured since communications were down anyhow, the odds of him getting into trouble were almost nil. He slid under the long gray panels, reached under the back and felt his way to the plug. At the exact same instance he plugged in the relay, the docks computer called for an internal communications test. The relay clicked, the transformer opened to let the high voltage through and the next thing he knew he was waking up about twelve feet from where he last remembered being. He stood up and staggered to the intercom box, reached up to call for help when he noticed that his finger nails were completely blown off his left hand.

  Every time he thought about this it reminded him that even a one in a million chance was too big a risk to take.

His thoughts returned to his present task. Flipping switches and tapping gauges until his pre-launch systems check was complete. With twenty minutes to spare he made his way to his berth for a power nap saying to himself. "I love it when a plan comes together."

Lewis finally emerged from his berth and made his way to the bridge. "How long are we scheduled to be docked at Gate 2?" He asked Jim Houtt who was running a diagnostic on the memory storage of the ship.

"Not quite sure, I'm guessing long enough for them to remove this redundant memory back up. Why do you ask?"

"Oh no reason in particular, it's we just left all that hoopla behind us now and I personally don't wish to run into Governor Trewer again."

"Chance of any of us running into the Governor will be pretty slim considering his butt will be in the fire at that summit. Wouldn't wanna be in his shoes, no sir eee bob." Houtt said as he started to whistle and went back to work.

"What you got going on there?" Lewis asked.

Houtt tapped the list that was given to him just before they launched. "Seems like every stop we make I have to pull some kind of something or other out of this ship and give it to whoever asks for it. Here at Gate 2 I'm unloading the ships entire redundant memory. This dates back to the first trip up until five minutes ago when I disconnected it. By the time we abandon this baby at Gate 6 it will be nothing but an outer shell. From what I gather security requires disassembling it in stages, this way no one person can alter the tugs path."

Lewis placed his list down on the console in front of him. "You get all the exciting stuff I see." He said to Houtt as he sat down at the main circuit board.

Jim Houtt had to crawl under the console to plug in and when he did Lewis took advantage of the situation and down loaded all the codes, serial numbers and passwords for the memory dumps. *Houtt won't miss these one bit,* he thought. *Probably will never even know I removed them.*

Jim Houtt pulled himself back out from under the console. "There, that's that." He said as he placed his needle nose pliers back in his tool box. "I can chill out for a few hours." Lewis gave Houtt a hand up to his feet before disappearing back to his quarters.

Miller was the new guy on the crew or low dog as the rest liked to call him. Along with making sure all pneumatic doors were sealed at the proper times and locations his most important job was to make sure the coffee pot was never seen empty. He didn't really fit the mold the other guys were cut from. Quieter than the others, he liked to be left alone and preferred to work that way too. Stocky from head to toe with a little extra in the middle he could carry his own weight in any situation, including a few toe to toe shouting matches he never backed down from, Thus earning him the respect from everyone else on board. He could feel the slight bump and nudge as Quincy moved the box into place. Garbage haulers or boxes were some halfwit's political answer to the disposal needs of the planet and its orbiting substations.

Twice a month a box would be sent on its journey to C - Gate 6. Once through the gate there was no turning around. The gates consisted of a magnetic acceleration and course guidance systems for anywhere in the universe. C gates were used for commercial business only and C - Gate 6 was the last manned outpost before a box was sent on its trajectory into the sun where it and its contents would be vaporized.

Docked in orbit around the Earth, The Barge Omega awaited as robot welders finished their 40 hour job of securing the box. With 24 hours to go, the remaining crew started to show up. Shooster, whose job it was to keep the debris from collecting on the docking ports and external locks, he stood almost six feet tall, with a protruding nose he unsuccessfully tried to hide with a moustache and close cropped salt and pepper hair. He had a tendency of self-indulgent posturing and running his mouth hundreds of miles an hour while his brain was sitting still with no chance whatsoever to catch up. Neanderthal by nature, dumb as a box of rocks often referring to himself in the third person. However he would be the first person you ask any question of, he always has the right answer.

Manetti, the oldest of the 5 man crew, was over due to retire. Why anyone that age would sign up for a 2 year. travel to C Gate 6 is beyond me; but, the real puzzle is why would Administration send him? Master mechanic and carpenter his skills are always welcome: however, the fact that he's as old as the space we travel in gives him a warped sense of authority. Whenever he went hunting he always shot the twelve point buck and every time he went fishing he always limited out and every time he went gambling he always won big money. He always flew private jets and was a personal guest of the best casino suites available....or so he said. Slightly bent at the knee made him look shorter than he really was. His job on board was mechanical construction and locksmith. Generous beyond expectations and given the right tools he can fix anything.

Miller and Shooster start checking systems and time tables, on the average the trip to C Gate 1 takes about 16 days.

The rhythm of the bump whirr bump whirr was all but hypnotic as Miller continued to load the circuits. The sun shining like a golden spoon engulfed the starboard side of the ship, the temperature was at least 100 degrees Celsius warmer on the sunny side. Miller closed the visors on the windows as he wheeled the boxes of supplies to the elevator. Once in the elevator, complete automation takes over and the next time any crew member sees the items now being placed in storage is when they are called up.

Shooster made his way down to the bottom of the ship. "It's like a sweat shop down here," he said to no one. Because no one but him ever ventures this deep. He was the only crew member on board who had a class D operator's license. In turn making him the only crew member on board with any business working in the deep recesses of the ship. Quincy 4 was still equipped with a series of six guidance cubes. Each cube acted independently of each other at the same time acting in series with each other. No small engineering feat here. If one cube failed that would cause the entire circuit to fail, the backup was five more. Many times in the past with this type of guidance system, the old tugs would be so far off course it was a miracle in and of itself, they never lost one and its crew to the sun.

He sat squat in a tiny cramped hole, bracing his back against the wall with just enough room to stretch out one leg in front of him. With a headlamp strapped to his backwards ball cap, he pulled the circuit breakers one by one, testing to see which breaker would shut down which cube. "This is totally insane," he held down the talk button on his radio. He wore a lapel microphone, finding it easier to talk without actually holding his radio in his hand. "Whoever came up with this idea should be shot. Here I sit, literally pulling the only guidance system this ship has and we have to surrender it at Gate 3?" His communication was heard by everyone else on the ship.

"Copy that Shoe." Miller the newest guy on the crew confirmed.

Nothing was in its original state but then again that was no surprise. When the system was installed circuit one went to cube one and respectively down the line. Over the decades however, the circuits and cubes became a jumbled guessing game. According to his list, he was to remove every cube except cube number five. Cube five was the communications cube. It handled all communications on board from the automatic coffee pot to deep space location. This meant no matter what, if the tug was off course, cube 5 would communicate to C-Gate 6 and close the gate as well as brew a fresh pot of coffee. Once in deep space your location is dependent on cube 5. It was normal operations during deep space travel to be hundreds of thousands of miles off course, it was expected. The guidance cube was the only functional method to regain a safe locatable course. Once turned on, the cube would emit a steady pulsating beacon consisting of micro waves and laser. (A cross between laser and radar.) When those waves bounced off a designated location, the ship in turn would redirect and set its new course. This procedure was known as closing the gate. It took Shooster about fourteen hours to run through every combination and when he emerged from the pit, he was muscling around a floor cart carrying one of the six cubes, measuring three feet square and weighing around eighty pounds. He sat the cube in the long dim hallway leading from the shaft to the air locks. There they awaited pick up at C-Gate 3.

Manetti and Houtt were sipping a cup of coffee standing there chuckling and making little comments watching Shooster work.

"Hey Shoe why did you remove those now instead of waiting til we get there?" Manetti asked him.

Shooster pulled the large envelope that was tucked in the back of his pants, handed it to Manetti.

"You tell me? First of all, why we have to remove them, and then tell me secondly why it has to be done on this time frame?" Shooster pointed to the schedule.

Manetti glanced at it then tilted the paper so Houtt could read it too. Both men stood there reading Shooster's schedule with bewilderment. Manetti looked up at Houtt, both have seen twice the number of tugs retired and not one required the removal of any of its systems.

"I'll wait here Shoe. You go drop the cubes and I'll stack them for pick up at the bay three doors," Manetti said.

"Sounds like a plan to me." He disappeared back down the shaft only to reemerge in about ten minutes with another cube.

Two days into the trip word had reached Governor Trewer about his son and the mess at his house. The good news was the blood and brains did not belong to his son. The bad news was the puke did.

"So what do they have as far as evidence from the scene?" Governor Trewer asked William via satellite communications.

"They got nothing from me boss," William said, then added, "But this is what I know. We have unidentified DNA in the home. Finger prints, some of which belong to of all people, Frank Lewis. The Yoman you put away..."

"Yes I know who Frank Lewis is, but why was he on the property? is the question. How soon until the third party DNA is returned from the lab?"

"Not a clue sir, Detective Miles was real keen on not letting me in on any of the details."

"Did you just say Detective Miles?"

"Yes sir. Detective Miles is running the whole investigation."

"Ok, listen to me close Moss."

William knew when he was called by his last name things were going to be serious.

"I need you to get a message to Chief Inspector Burns. Get a pen and paper and write down exactly what I tell you, verbatim, understand?"

"Yes sir, I'm ready when you are."

"Dear Chief Inspector Burns, it has been brought to my attention you have Detective Brandon Miles leading the investigation on my property. I would like to take a moment to remind you that Detective Miles is twenty months into a twenty four month restraining order, barring him from entering my property. If you will remember correctly, Detective Miles illegally entered my property and willfully caused destruction to several windows and doors trying to enter my home. I understand the seriousness of your investigation; however, I will be requesting a cease and desist order from Judge Knight and a request to close the investigation sighting you and Detective Miles."

The Governor paused for a second. "I guess that's all I have for now."

"And I'm guessing it will be enough sir," William chimed in. I'll get this message out within the minute Governor."

"William?" the Governor asked.

"Yes sir?"

"There is absolutely no sign of Kester anywhere"?

"No sir, as best I can figure out, he left the scene in one of the cars and even the police missed that fact. He's run off before sir and the scene here is pretty bad. Let's just keep the thoughts positive and hope he went somewhere to lay low for a while."

Both men knew Kester was not smart enough to lay low. More likely than not, if he was still alive he was stoned in some alley somewhere in town.

The sat line went dead. Bill Moss vowed under his breath, if he finds Kester before the authorities do, he'll break both his legs.

Week 4

Miller stepped into the main control room of Quincy 4. Houtt was in his usual seat pushing buttons and playing old video games.

"Seems like this is all our computer will do for us now," he said as he turned to watch Miller walk in. Miller was an average size man sporting a heavy goatee and a ponytail that were blonde in days gone by. Today he was wearing some old camouflage hat he picked up at who knows where.

"What's on your agenda today?" Houtt asked. Adding, "Week 4 and you finally show yourself. We thought maybe you stayed behind."

"Yeah well you know how it is around here. The less I see of certain people the better off I am." Miller turned to the gray console to his left flipped a few switches and started taking oxygen level and temperature readings.

"Can I just squeeze in behind you?" he asked Jim.

"No problem, what you got going on today?"

"Well according to my instructions, today we start circulating our oxygen supply through the garbage." He said with a smile.

"You can't be serious?" Houtt replied.

"Not only am I serious but I'm also a little confused about this whole thing. I never really experienced Co2 filtering before. I figured it was a lost art of survival. According to my calculations our in house oxygen levels will be borderline red zone by the time we get off this dinosaur. And... having said that I'm sure we will be quite acclimated to the odiferous conditions. Heck, we probably won't even know the whole place smells like garbage."

Houtt could only shake his head.

"Yeah I know man, sucks to be us huh? They spared no savings on this journey. Maybe we should go over each other's instructions sometime soon, so we know exactly what's in store for us. Gonna be a long haul I'm afraid ... and yes the pun was intended. In the meantime, the temperature inside the barge should be between sixty and eighty five degrees."

Houtt gave Miller a quizzical look.

"Hey man, it's like a terrarium in there. We pump in the Co2 then the moss and mold turn it back to oxygen, then we pump it back out for us to breath. Combine that with our on board supply of oxygen and we're good to go."

Miller pulled the key that was in his instruction envelope out of his pocket. Unlocked the four small silver locks one at each corner of the console, grabbed the handles and pulled it straight up. Inside was a series of solenoids, switches and mechanical valves.

"Here goes nothing." He started to open the valves and then disconnect the solenoids so they would stay open. Immediately two things took place. The first was Houtt turned to Miller and asked. "Did you just fart?" As the entire cabin area started to smell like rotten garbage. The second thing that happened was Kester Trewer took another shallow breath only this time it was cleaner oxygen.

Meantime, Lewis needed to find out where Manetti and Shooster put the cubes but didn't want to just come right out and ask. He decided to go on a little expedition of his own. He figured if he checked all the bays he would sooner or later find what he was looking for. He managed to go undetected to the loading bay. Just about every bay was empty. A few console covers here and there that had been removed by Shooster and Miller. The only closed bay door was bay three. "Bingo!" Lewis whispered, and made his way to bay four to check the adjacent door. It was unlocked which meant it was not coded for entry which meant easy access which meant Lewis had plenty of time to act. C-Gate 3 was still weeks away. He pulled the security access card from bay four and slipped it in his pocket. As long as bay four was unlocked and the adjoining door to bay three was unlocked, he would have no problem carrying out his task. And no one would be the wiser.

With C-Gate 3 still a few weeks out Manetti figured it was time for a little fun. He cornered Shooster and showed him a gag he was about to play on Lewis. He held in his hand an expandable cloth. One they would use to clean up large spills.

"Check this out Shoe, I dunked this cloth in mechanics grease. After I flush it, I'll tell Frank the toilets plugged up. By the time he gets all the pipes apart looking for the plug, the grease will have disintegrated the rag. He'll spend days looking for a clog that don't exist."

"Oh you're one rotten old man Manetti. He gave Manetti a fist bump and walked away. An hour later Lewis was seen lugging his plumber's bag to the lower decks of the ship.

Back on Earth

William Moss had managed to squelch the presses interest in what took place at the Governor's mansion. He held a press release of his own and promised any further leaks of the incident would be dealt with executively. For the press, at least to the veterans, this meant the story was now off limits. No ifs, ands or buts about it. Detective Miles gave him a clean report after he checked out William's alibi. The investigation was still ongoing though and the house was still off limits.

William decided to do a little investigation of his own. He started back at Fu Young for lunch then headed into the seedy underground of China Town. Kester had been forcefully removed from a few of the opium dens William knew about, and probably a few he didn't. He walked down the alley behind the restaurant and knocked on a big gray steel door with stains of rust smeared in a runny pattern. A small Chinese woman answered the door. She looked like she may have weighed a whopping ninety pound in combat boots. She puffed her silver hair from her scornful face.

"Go away, we not open!" She said in a squeaky little voice through crooked yellow teeth.

William knocked again.

This time the door was opened more than just a crack and a tall thin Chinese man stood there with a homemade weapon of wood and nails in his hand. William could see the small woman standing behind him. She was missing her left arm and looked like to William she was the victim of her own poison. The man holding the weapon recognized him and motioned for him to enter. He stepped inside and was met with a growl and look of disgust from the woman. He just smiled at her and walked into the den. Immediately hit with the smell of body odor, sex, opium and death. It took away all his senses at once. He asked the man if he had seen Kester and when the man said no, he asked if he could take a look himself.

"Five minit you got, only five minit then you go." The one armed little old lady told him.

William detected a slight smile of satisfaction on the old woman's face and headed deep into the bowels of the opium den. Kester was nowhere to be found. On his way out he palmed the man some cash and nodded in gratitude. He walked another block to another den. He knew the drill by now, all the dens were networked together. If you got tossed out of one you would not be allowed in another. When William knocked on the second door the man there was already holding his hand out for payment. He was a little friendlier than the last man.

"You like a pipe while you look for your friend?" he asked William in a high pitched voice. William just brushed past him and went inside. He could hear the man saying." I remember you. Yes, yes, yes, I remember you. You big money man. You spend all your money right here ok?" The man anxiously tried to position himself in front of William. "You spend money here in my place, yes, ok mister?"

William brushed past the man and continued his search. Again no sign of Kester not even a prospect of him ever being there. Two more blocks over he knocked on a third door. This time another woman answered.

"Look!" she said. "We know who your friend is. And he no be in China Town. You understand? If he was here we would know. Now stop being fool with your money and go. Leave China Town now. You knock on no more doors mister, ok? "

William knew this was his last warning. If he was not buying he was not welcome and it was time for him to go. He handed the old woman a picture of Kester, she handed it back to him.

"I told you mister, we know who you look for. He not in China Town ever! Now go!" She raised her voice and pointed sternly to the alley. When William stepped out into the alley he was met by six members of the Dragon Clan, the opium security guards. They politely escorted him the four blocks back to his car, punched him in his stomach then spray painted a big green X on the side of his car and left him doubled over on the ground. This ended William's search for Kester Trewer ... At least in China Town.

7 weeks earlier

Lewis could not be any happier about being in the sub levels of the ship. This put him within feet of the remaining guidance cube. He knew the rest of the crew was laughing behind his back about the plugged up toilet but figured the last laugh would be on him. The guidance cube held the ship on course and it also housed the redundant safety system. The system that automatically closed C-gate 6 when the ship was off course and then re-direct it. All he had to do was replace that cube with any one of the discarded five from bay 3 and then wait for A.M.P., to be initiated then he was home free. If he timed it right A.M.P. would occur just days before their arrival at C-Gate 3.

Kester Trewer managed to open an eye. His mind panicked. "*Where am I?*" He wondered. He looked in all the directions his open eye would allow, and then it dawned on him he was laying on top the garbage in the barge Omega 1. He wondered how long he'd been unconscious. His chest hurt where the electrical prod zapped him and mobility was all but nonexistent. He wondered why he wasn't dead.

Without warning a chill hit and his stomach cramped causing involuntary spasms. "*This can't be real,*" he thought. "*I'm going through withdraws?!*" His surroundings became secondary with this awakening of terror. A junkie's greatest fear, going through withdraws alone. Another violent spasm caused his body to curl in the fetal position. He broke out in a cold shiver, there was little fluid in his body for sweat. His mouth was dry, his fingers were bent to the inside of his palms, and all his body's tendons tightened up causing him to be immobile. The next spasm that rocked through his body shook him so violently he rolled onto his other side causing his head to snap back so fast in a rapid whiplash motion he briefly lost consciousness. When he came to this time his face was resting against the cool side of the barge. For what little comfort that offered he was grateful. He felt something cold and wet trickle down his cheek. At first he thought it was blood from his head, then realized it was too cold. He stuck his tongue out to taste it.

"*Water? How can that be?*" He wondered. It tasted foul, almost rancid but he laid there reeling in pain and spasms licking the condensation from the wall of the barge. He could feel his body start to absorb the hydration.

On deck Houtt opened the communications channel to the whole ship. "Ok every one listen up. Due to the summit on C-gate 2 we were just given a pass. A drone will meet up with us before Gate 3 to seize the memory banks, the 5 cubes and the ships logs. And just for the record, it was them not me who used the word seize. Once the drone picks up the package we'll be given a green light protocol to increase our speed. Next stop C-Gate 4. Countdown to A.M.P. begins now.

Chapter 5

C-Gate3

(A.M.P.)

A.M.P. Automatic Memory Process. This is a memory over ride discovered entirely by accident when a college student inadvertently ran a memory over itself. He discovered that his memory was completely wiped clean from his hard drive. No part of it left behind. It just vanished into thin air. The world's governments quickly realized the advantage of using this to their own advantage. They also realized the disadvantage of the public using it. In 2212 this procedure became the standard for all governments and military and quickly became outlawed to all civilians.

Manetti and Lewis both approached Houtt at the same time. He was sitting on the bridge playing a computer game on the large screen.

Manetti spoke first, "Did you really just say, we're not docking at Gate 3?"

Houtt paused his game, typed a few words on the keyboard in front of him.

"Look for yourself."

The message read something like this: Due to security reasons, we have initiated protocol for your vessel to bypass C-Gate 3. You will rendezvous with a UPV (automatic piloted vehicle) at which time a representative from the company will board you and assist in the removal of selected electronic components. Your next scheduled stop will now be C-Gate 4.

"Figures," Manetti said. "I was seriously thinking about surrendering my bonus and heading home. I'm just getting too old for this crap."

"Sorry my friend, this is what happens when you become a company man. We have about ten days before we hook up. Don't know about you, but I'm gonna sleep for a week." Having said that, he picked up the ships intercom and announced to whoever cared, he was going down for a week.

Frank Lewis stood behind the two men and listened in total disbelief. He too was thinking about getting off the ship at C-Gate 3. However his destination was not back on Earth, his plans were to stay as far away from Earth as he could. He said nothing, wandering back to his quarters feeling sick to his stomach again. Following suit with everyone else on board he climbed in his sarcophagus and didn't re-emerge for a week.

Four days and counting until the entire memory of Quincy 4 will no longer exist. Manetti plopped down in a chair in Shooster's quarters.

"I think someone is going through a lot of trouble to erase this mission from the analogs of history," he said as he rubbed his bald head. He looked up at Shoe, grinned and with a chuckle added, "makes me wonder if we'll ever see home again, just a gut feeling I have."

Just then Houtt walked passed the room, poked his head in and asked, "meeting of the minds guys?"

Shooster pointed to a chair. "Have a seat my good old fat buddy, maybe we need to talk about this."

Jim Houtt sat down. "Ok I'm all ears."

"Well Vince here," he pointed to Manetti. "Has some concerns and frankly I do too. You realize by the time we get to Gate 4 this ship will only be guided by one out of six cubes, it will have no memory, we're sucking recycled oxygen from the garbage and we won't be able to contact anyone at home in time to stop us."

Jim Houtt shook his head. "Sheesh, you mean to tell me you guys are falling for this crap?" He took off his glasses, wiping his forehead. "The reason for the cubes is obvious. They can be used anywhere on just about anything. This isn't the first time anyone here has AMP'ed. We do it all the time. It's just a security thing. As far as sucking in recycled air, wish I had better news about that one, you might be right. They're gonna poison us with polluted air. Ask yourselves this, what purpose does it serve to get rid of us?" He left the room shaking his head.

"I'm still not buying it." Manetti said walking out. He turned to Shooster, "another thing, I think we need to keep a close eye on that weasel Frank too."

Shooster's door whooshed shut behind Manetti and he was met in the corridor by Jim Houtt.

"What's the matter with you?" He asked Manetti with a hint of booze on his breath. "Every time you gotta stir the pot don't you? You couldn't keep this to yourself? We have a mission to run and yeah, I've added two plus two and got three as well. Someone on this ship knows something and I'm guessing it's our plumber; but, until I know for sure, you keep your trap shut got it?"

All Manetti could do was stand there and put up with it. "I'll go tell Shoe to keep quiet," He said.

"You'll do no such thing, just leave it alone now, the less attention we bring the better off we are." He turned and walked away and then spoke over his shoulder. "By the way my personal password became invalid today, I was issued a new one, and I can't change it, better check yours."

Kester was still shaking violently. The rancid water gave him back some painful mobility. There was a distant glow of red from where was laying. He focused on the light for a minute trying to figure out what it was. His right hand was closed tight in a fist and his legs were numb. His shirt was burned into his chest from the electrical prod and he could only open one eye. He surmised they were still docked on Earth because the temperature was not subzero and there was breathable oxygen. His stomach hurt from the spasms and felt like it was inside out. He started to dry heave making it hurt worse. When he finally managed to free his right arm from under his body and raise it to his head, his hand was clenched tight in a fist. He slowly opened it. To his astonishment he found he was holding on tightly to a baggie of drugs Yoman gave him just before he zapped him with the electrical prod. He gasped a small laugh of disbelief. Some of his supply was crushed into a fine dusting of powder from being involuntarily clenched in his fist so tight. Another spasm bent his body so perversely his knees were now pursed against his lips. He needed to relieve himself of the withdrawals and quickly. In the dark, with only the faint red glow somewhere off in the distance he laid the baggie next to his chest. *"Easy Kester, you can't afford to drop this."* His mind was racing, his body was growing tighter, his temperature was rising and his fever was high. With excruciating pain he unfurled his fingers a little more. His hand shaking like he was waving goodbye to an old friend, he wrapped his forefinger and middle finger around the top of the baggie. He could hear the thin plastic crackle as the baggie shook now as violently as he was. *"Careful."* He thought. The baggie flipped and flopped in the air just inches from his face while it tumbled down with a snap. He still had it pinched between his two fingers which had become so unsteady causing his mind to freak out a little more. With his two remaining fingers and his thumb, he slid the plastic folds to a position where he could slide a finger inside. He did and managed to collect a little of the fine dust coating the inside of the baggie. Just as he removed his hand another violent spasm wracked him so painfully he lost his grasp on the baggie, it disappeared in the vast wasteland he now called home. He tried to raise his powder covered fingers to his mouth but his arm would not cooperate. From his good eye he could see his hand shaking just inches from his face. *"Come on, please just a few inches."* With a desperate begging hum he stuck his tongue out as far as he could. Still could not reach his fingers. *So close I can smell it."* Another spasm pulled his body closer into itself only this time it worked out to his advantage and he could reach his fingers with his tongue. His mouth was dry and the powder was bitter, he tried to suck it off his fingers but he had no saliva left. He finally succumbed to another spasm and blacked out again. With no understanding of how much time passed, when he finally came to, his body was a little more relaxed. Still shaking violently, he pulled himself up to a sitting position and started to lap the condensation from the wall again. *"Just when you think you have sunk as low as you can,"* he thought. He broke out in a hysterical laughter that ended up in a hysterical sobbing. He then tried to assess his damaged body. The burn on his chest from what he could see was second and third degree burns. His skin was open and his shirt was stuck to the wound. He felt his face next. His left eye was open his right eye just felt like a huge blister. He found dried blood coming from both ears, his shoulder was dislocated and what he feared the most had come true, his left leg was broken, a compound fracture that luckily did not break the skin, however he could feel his shin bone and the separation. He figured he was a dead man as soon as the barge entered orbit and frantically began looking for the lost baggie.

Lewis called Shooster from the sublevel of the tug.

"Hey Shooie think you can give me hand down here?"

"What do you need?" Shooster asked.

"Well I have this auxiliary main pump line taken apart and I need someone or something to hold it up while I reattach it."

"I'll be down there in five minutes." Shooster said with a monotone voice which indicated he really didn't want to go. The sublevel door opened and Shooster stepped in.

"What kind of mess you into now?" He looked at all the pipes and brackets dismantled on the floor. "You gotta be joking? You took all this apart to find a plugged up toilet?"

Lewis just laughed. "All you have to do is hold those pipes in place while I band the brackets back around them. Three hours and we're finished."

"Yeah, well I want some of what you're drinking cause I got news for you, I'm not touching this job, you're on your own."

Lewis dropped the pipe. "The toilet was easy, I just happen to stumble on the leak while I was down here. You've done these lines before. You know the only way to fix it is to dismantle it from end to end. If you aint gonna help me then at least find something I can rest the pipes on to hold them in place so I can band em."

He pointed to the work bench. "I'll give you a hand bringing the work bench over maybe you can use that."

"Nope no good, I already measured it. The work bench is four and a half feet tall and I need something about three feet tall... or someone to stand here and hold them."

"I already told you, I'm not touching this cluster, let me see what I can find."

When Shooster returned with one of the guidance cubes on a flat cart Lewis thought. *"Man that was too easy."* He was proud of himself for the way that played out. However he was not as proud as Shooster was solving the dilemma.

"I guess these cubes paid off since I had to remove them." He wheeled the flat cart next to Lewis.

"It goes back to bay 3 when you're finished ..." With a wave of his hand over the back of his head as he walked out and was gone.

Lewis wasted no time switching out the cubes. Quincy 4 no longer had its safeguard and once they A.M.P.'ed even the memory of a safeguard on board the ship would be gone. Next on his list, Hackjack the system.

Being bored, Manetti sat down at the main control panel and started to go through a series of system checks. He figured it would give him something to do. Oxygen levels checked out good. Some of the stench from filtering their air through the garbage finally subsided. Temperatures in the barge were a steady 65 degrees due to the warm air being filtered in. Manetti turned on the infrared scan and to his amusement he found they had a stow away on board.

"Check it out," he said to Houtt and Shooster who were enjoying a cup of coffee on the bridge.

"We got us a live one and by the looks of things he's a big un too." The other two men took a look.

"How do you know it's an animal?" Houtt asked

"Could be something fermenting I suppose, possible prelude to spontaneous combustion. But look here and then look over there. You see those other orange spots?" Manetti was pointing to his screen. "They look the same in color only smaller. I'll keep an eye on em and see if they move. Besides it's not like I have anything else to do.

Lewis finished up switching out the cube and putting the pipes back together when Shooster met him in the corridor. "Want some help with stacking that cube?" He asked Lewis.

"Naw man, I think I can manage it from here. It worked out perfect too, I might add." With that Lewis started pushing the flat cart back to bay 3. He stopped dead in his tracks when Shooster said. "By the way Frank, it looks like we got a live one in the barge. Imagine that. And just think it'll be slow cooking all the way to the sun."

Lewis walked back to Shooster. "Say that again, did you just tell me there is something living in the garbage?"

"Yep a few something's according to the infrared scan we just looked at."

"It's not uncommon. Is it a dog?"

"Seems to be a little bigger. Vince, Jim and I saw it. Take a look for yourself when you get that cube unloaded. I'll meet you up there. I wanna get a better look at it too."

Lewis had to hold his composure and Shooster couldn't see the nervous look on his face as he walked away from him. Twenty minutes later all four men were looking at the infrared scans on a large monitor screen.

"Whatever the big one is, it must be pretty injured because it barely moves at all. I counted over a dozen of the small critters. At least I'm guessing they're critters by the way they scurry around. Rats most likely. This is a first for me, usually anything living freezes to a Popsicle as soon as we breaks Earth's orbit," Manetti said.

"This is impossible," said Houtt. "We've been in space for weeks now and we only recently started pumping warm air there. That has to be some nonliving heat source. Some spontaneous heat source, even those little ones you think are rats must be something else. Something that thawed out and started rotting causing a heat exchange."

Lewis had nothing to say. He inconspicuously wiped the sweat from his forehead then went back to his quarters and pulled up the infrared scan on his personal screen.

"I'll be switched," he muttered to himself. "How on Earth did you manage to survive?"

He just sat there for hours on end staring at the screen in amazed bewilderment. Every now and then he would utter the word "impossible" and go back to watching the screen.

Jim Houtt who seemed unaffected by all this went back to his quarters too and turned on the infrared scan on his personal screen. "What in the name of Sam is going on on this ship? If I didn't know any better I would swear we have a living person in that dumpster." He got out his log and started to make an entry describing the events of the last few weeks. One by one he started to list all that seemed suspect. There wasn't a clear pattern, a mystery to him so he started to thumb backwards through his journal and there he found the missing part of the puzzle. "*It was Lewis who opened the air vents as soon as Quincy and the Omega barge were connected. He immediately started pumping warm air from Quincy into the barge but why?*" Houtt left his quarters and buzzed Lewis in his.

"Yeah, what can I do for you?"

"Need to have a word with you, it's important," Houtt answered.

"Hold on a sec, be right there." Lewis turned off the infrared scan and brought the plumbing schematic up on his screen. He opened his door and invited Jim in.

"What's up?" Lewis asked.

Houtt placed his daily log on the table and pointed to the entry dated the moment they connected to the barge.

"This is what's up? I have you located in sublevels of this ship just as we locked on to this barge. According to the computer files I documented, which of course, no longer exist at least on this ship. Anyhow this log shows you opened the panel and turned the positive air flow on. Can you explain this?"

"I was double checking the system is all, I thought I was closing em." Lewis couldn't look Houtt in the face giving that answer.

"First of all Frank, that was Miller's job. You're not supposed to be on that level of the ship..." He was interrupted by Lewis.

"Let's get something straight Jim, this is a union boat and this is a union job. I can and will go wherever I please whenever I please you got that? It was an honest mistake," he concluded.

Houtt walked away and Lewis could hear him say. "It was a mistake alright, but I'm bettin it wasn't very honest."

Lewis sat on the edge of his table, placed his head in his hands and cursed himself for such a stupid screw up. He has no one but himself to blame for any life in that barge. The mystery still remained how anyone or anything stayed alive during the first four hours before the warm air was pumped in.

Houtt buzzed Miller next. It took a while for him to answer. He opened the door to let Houtt in his quarters. He had a paint pallet and a brush in his hand. Houtt walked in, looked around and started to laugh at Miller's quarters.

"You gonna paint the whole room?" He asked. "Now I know why no one's seen you for days."

"I got nothing but time and sixteen gallons of paint I managed to stow before we left. What's up?" Miller responded, holding his artists thumb up as a joke.

"I just spoke with Lewis and he claims he inadvertently opened the positive air dampers to the barge thinking he was closing them. You did close them before we left, right?"

"Yep not only did I close em but I tagged em too."

"There were no tags on those valves when I checked em."

"You mean we never reopened them? They've been open this whole time?"

"Kind of looks that way, let me show you what Vince stumbled on earlier today when he was bored." Houtt turned on Millers personal screen and switched it to the infrared scan.

"You see this?" He pointed to the screen.

Miller walked over and leaned closer to the screen. "We have someone alive in the barge? That's impossible."

"At this point no one is calling that someone, but it is something alive. Along with all those little something's which we think are rats." Houtt told him.

Miller was still looking at the infrared image when it started to move. "It's moving and it sure looks like a person to me."

Houtt took another look, "it sure does doesn't it?" He straightened up and saluted Miller in a playful military way. "Carry on Picasso, and I think a splash of blue will look good over there on that wall," and then walked out.

By now anyone who was watching the infrared scan thought the same thing. They have a stowaway in the garbage. And everyone was asking the same question. "*What are we going to do about it?*"

Kester was frantic, his relief from being doubled over and wracked with pain was not going to last. He had no clue how long he'd been balled up in the fetal position. All he knew was he needed to locate his baggie of dope before he found himself in that condition again. His arms and wrists hurt from being tucked under his body. The tendons in both legs have contracted so severely drawing them high into his chest. Slowly he ignored everything else and winced with pain as he made an attempt to stretch them out. Guided only by his sense of feel, he grit his teeth and screamed out loud, forcing his good leg to straighten out. Next his fingers. He opened both hands just a little, let the agony subside before repeating that motion. His fingers were stiff, the pain was sharp and stabbing. Each knuckle grinding at a snail's pace until his fingers were completely outstretched. Working them back and forth from a fist to an extended hand, from there he worked on his wrists, again working them back and forth until they moved with less pain and effort. He extended an arm and found the edge of something bulky and covered with a soft material. It was an old discarded sofa, locking his finger under the lip he managed to pull himself forward about a foot. When he tried to pull himself forward the second time, the sofa started to slide pulling him with it. He scraped his chest across the many undetermined items of garbage and trash, each one clawing and sanding away like a bastard metal rasp on the opened wound in his chest. He wanted to let go, he needed to let go, yet he couldn't let go. His fingers locked in place under the sofa, he was along for the ride. It seemed for just a second the downward travel stopped, then like in some comedic movie in the annals of his memory he teetered on the brink of the abyss before tumbling over the edge.

He bounced. He twisted. He slid. He fell. He tumbled. One moving piece of garbage led to another being dislodged, an avalanche of trash. Cans collecting busted end tables smearing through rotten food rolling across discarded clothing moving in waves before him, followed by cascading cushions, empty boxes and boards with nails sticking up. He screamed in pain, he gasped in horror and finally came to rest in the cold dark bowels of the garbage tug known as Omega. His body was like one great big raw nerve. With every movement it felt like an electric shock shooting through his entire being. He felt around his new surroundings on the off chance his bag of dope was nearby. The surface was hard, made of what he thought might be some type of building material. The sofa landed upside down and luckily the cushions were close. Rolling over on his side, he pushed against the slime with his good foot while clawing with his hands until he reached the sofa. Moved the cushions to form a soft place to rest making a small cave. He crawled inside and collapsed from exhaustion.

He came to with a little bit of clarity, laying there in his little sofa cave. Bits and pieces of recollection started to form a solid memory. Porter was dead and he was left for dead in the garbage, both by the hand of Yoman Frank Lewis. He remembered the shooting. He remembered the ride to the sweeps. He remembered being zapped. He kept playing back the events in his head, each time was clearer than the last. He remembered Porter trying to reason with Lewis. He remembered yelling at Lewis. He remembered Lewis handing him a gun then threatening to pin the murder on him. He remembered Lewis giving him a bag of dope to quiet him down. He remembered stuffing the dope deep into a cargo pocket on his right leg. *Do I still have the dope?* He wondered. With a hand that reminded him of a cripple, he slide it down his pant leg. The snap on his pocket was hard for him to undo with his fingers bent the way they were. He managed to curl his index finger around the brass colored snap and forced it to pop open. Reaching in his pocket he finally felt the crinkle of the thin plastic baggie. In the pitch black surroundings of his sofa cave, he ingested a few more pills and waited for his buzz to kick in.

Two days later a digital message was sent to Earth from Quincy 4. The message was in code and the recipient was unknown at this point. Miller just happened to be digitizing files of the new art work that now adorned his quarters when the message left via his personal communication block. Each berth was equipped with its own communications box. So why was his the one that sent the message? Miller called Houtt and asked him to stop in his quarters.

"What's up?" Houtt asked.

"Well if we really do have a live person in the garbage, I'm betting someone back home now knows about it. Personally I would like to know what's happening." He turned his infrared scan back on just to take another look. The image was gone. Houtt checked Miller's digital records.

"Yep something just left here for Earth. You have no idea what it said or where it originated?"

"Not a clue" said Miller. "Like I told you I was digitizing the pictures I took." He motioned with his hand to the surrounding unfinished art work that decorated his entire quarters. "It had to originate on board, chances are it was sent to all of our blocks and sent out. This way there's no tellin who sent it originally."

"Well, it's obvious we have a serious situation on our hands," Houtt said as he glanced at the infrared scan, too. "Looks gone to me, whatever it was and movement was limited at best when we did see it. I think when we dock at Gate 4 we should find some help. What do you think?"

"I think you're right and I also think until we do dock we keep this to ourselves."

Two hours later Miller came back to see Houtt, he carried his folder with his instructions inside. Manetti and Lewis were both watching the infrared with Houtt when Miller handed him his large manila envelope. On the front of the envelope he wrote. *"We just got a message back."*

"Time for me to take a break," Houtt announced to the other two men. He turned to Miller, "buy you a cup of coffee?"

The two men then walked into the kitchen together.

"Did the message only come to your computer?" he asked Miller.

"No idea maybe everyone got it? I deciphered it, three words. *Never on Wednesday"*

Miller shrugging his shoulders. "No idea what it means. Ok let's take a look at my computer and see if I got anything."

They headed towards Houtt's quarters and sure enough he had a red blinking light indicating a message waiting for him too. Three sets of numbers a set of four a set of two and a set of nine. "Pretty simple code if you ask me, mine says the same. *Never On Wednesday"*

Lewis was not aware his incoming message was received by everyone on the ship when he checked to see if it had arrived. Just as he suspected, when he broke down the number sets to letters it would read, *Never On Wednesday.* He took the first letter of each word and that was his message from Earth. *NOW.* Without hesitation he plugged into the ships main computers. With the memory removed this should be pretty simple he thought. The program was already written and all he had to do was run it. And that's exactly what he did. As a side enterprise on Earth, Lewis carried out a few hackjacks as well as a couple on a small scale in space, for the sole purpose of smuggling.

Essentially a hackjack is just what it sounds like. It's a hacked computer and hijacked vehicle. This allowed the hijacker to operate in a stealth mode, creating an invisible existence. Unless physical sight or contact is made, a ship can move through space virtually undetectable. Getting caught in a Hackjacked ship however, was cause for execution on the spot, usually carried out by ejecting the hackjacker from the ship.

In this case it was Quincy 4 that was hackjacked. Just seconds before he did this the ship received another message. This time it came from C-Gate 4. Manetti read it and picked up the mic and turned on the ships intercom.

"We just received a message from C-Gate 4 everyone. Who among us would believe it if I said we're not to stop and they'll send a drone to pick up the cubes?"

"Talk about your fast track." Houtt thought as he left his quarters to round up everyone.

All five men were gathered in the galley of the ship, no one was saying a word. Everyone just sat there waiting for the next person to speak.

"What's all this about?" Lewis finally spoke up.

Manetti crossed the room and got in Lewis' face and demanded. "You tell us, what this is all about!"

"You're crazy if you think I'm gonna stand here and let you sling accusations at me. I know just as much, if not less, than the rest of you." Lewis tried not to look suspicious or nervous. "Who got the message we're not docking at Gate 4?"

Manetti said, "It was me and I'll go you one further, when we get to Gate 5 I'm retired. This old man has played his last game in space. You guys can have it. I have a wife, kids and grandkids to get back to. No bonus is big enough to keep me here. This mission stinks. It stunk from the moment the decision to send this baby to the Sun was made. We gave up the ships memory at Gate 2!" His voice was getting louder. "Who does that? I have never in my life as crewman heard of surrender a ships memory so early into the mission. Matter of fact, I have never heard of it period. Oh sure, each one of us was given assignments and each one of us was given those hefty bonuses. I should have smelled a rat when I saw the amount. But no, stupid me, just figured I was getting that much because of my years of dedication." He rubbed his bald head with both hands and started to leave.

"Sorry Vince," Houtt said. "I can't let you leave just yet. You're absolutely right something smells like a rat here. I too have been keeping a close eye on things, entering everything in my log." Houtt being the senior man on board was in charge of the ships log, most of it was done electronically through the ships computer, at least up until now. "I have every entry in my log starting from the moment I sat down for preflight check. I have every record of every door, every hatch, and every panel, including every time someone flushed a toilet right here in my log."

What Houtt didn't realize was from the moment Lewis Hackjacked the ship, his log didn't mean squat to anyone but him. There was no information being sent out and no information coming in. Every communication was now on a loop being fed from a derelict ship. The Sandra K. docked at Gate 3 waiting to be salvaged. For all intents and purposes Quincy 4 just vanished from sight. No one on board would figure out the communications loop until it was too late and no one on Gate 3 would figure out The Sandra K. was really Quincy 4 and that Quincy 4 was really The Sandra K. Due to the fact Quincy 4's memory was gone and the guidance cubes would be removed, no one would be looking for her until Gate 4 which is still several weeks out.

Kester was foraging through the garbage trying to find something else to eat. *Maybe this time I'll find something decomposed and poisoned enough to finally do me in,* he thought. He wasn't quite sure if it was good fortune to find something to eat or not. He only had limited space to work in since he could hardly move and it took forever to regain enough strength to even worry about eating.

In his sickened state he didn't much care anymore, considering withdraws would be coming soon and he could only hope the next thing he found to eat was better than the last. With no light this deep in the barge he had to rely on touch and smell. He ran his scraped, cut up hands through some pretty disgusting stuff before he found what was left of some pastries. Sweet and moldy in a box, nonetheless he took a bite. Managing to keep it down he ate whatever he could get past his nose. Reluctant to move away from his water source in fear of not finding another he made the decision to make his way back up and towards the red light to see if there was a way out. His plan was to take the long way and stay close to the wall. Crawling through the garbage slowly on his hands and knees, progress was tedious as he had to feel his way around. Nothing seemed as it should be. Cardboard boxes collapsed under his weight. His hands fell through holes and his legs could not find perches to support him. He started to slide down again. If he reached the bottom of the barge he most likely would never make his way back up.

Something unidentifiable caught his shirt, ripping it open, exposing his infected burn. He could smell his own rotten skin and again wondered why he should bother to stay alive. By the time he stopped sliding downward he figured he must have gone another ten feet. There was nothing for him to climb back up with and even if there were, he didn't have the strength left in his arms to pull himself up. Slithering like a snake inches at a time he started to move the busted up decaying obstacles out of his way. He moved his hand forward and placed it in some rotten fruit. His hand slid through like grease and he started to gag. He could smell it now since he disturbed it.

"Peaches." He thought. *"Must be an entire load of rotten peaches."* The pile of peaches stood in his direct path. There was no way around them without going further down in the barge. He took time to pause to consider if going over the pile was really an acceptable option. He reached out his arm again and started to pat his hand around the area he was in. Still nothing but rotten fruit in every direction.

Kester laid there for several hours working up the gumption to start crawling through it. Then without warning he reached an arm out, kicked with his good leg then started to pull his way through. Once he broke the seal of the skins there was an explosion of putrid stench. He gagged and heaved but there was nothing in his stomach to come up. The smell was everywhere. His hand moved through it like he was swimming, and just like swimming he started to sink. Maggots! Millions of them! His mind panicked as he started to flay his arms and leg. The more he moved the quicker he sank. He stopped moving and waited to see what was going to happen next. Soon he stopped sinking too but he could barely get his head above the quicksand of garbage. Breathing heavily, he tried again to pull himself through. His hand landed on something long round and hard. It was a pipe of some kind. He grabbed it and prayed it wouldn't let go.

Slowly he dragged himself through the rotten fruit. Ducking his head forward like he was going to use his head as a battering ram, into the pile of peaches he went. He pulled himself in deeper and could feel the pressure of hundreds of pounds of slimy, rotten, maggot infested peaches pushing in on him. His eyes burned and he could taste the sweet rancid fermented wine on his lips. He could feel the maggots wriggling about on his face as he slowly and methodically plowed his way through.

At this point he guessed he dropped another ten to fifteen feet. Finding his way up to the surface now was pretty much a lost cause. He dragged himself along, carefully using the pipe as leverage. He reached a point where he thought was about six feet out of the fruit pile when he could feel nothing in front of him. The pipe extended out over thin air. How far? He was afraid to venture a guess. He pulled hand over hand on the pipe until he reached his center of balance but could still feel nothing. He sensed a vast cavernous area just below him and could actually feel the air being cooler. When he tried to back up on the pipe, it was so slippery from the fruit on his clothes he lost his grip and fell through the hole. He must have dropped about five feet and when he landed he could feel the bone in his leg press against his skin, thankfully it didn't puncture through. He managed to pull himself up to a sitting position and lean against something soft and much to his surprise, somewhat comfortable. Off to his left and not far away he heard a steady drip, which he hoped was the steady drip of water. He would investigate it later but for now he was completely exhausted and needed to rest. First things first he removed his rotten fruit soaked clothes and laid there in his underwear panting in agony.

"Drone will be here in two hours," Houtt informed Shooster. "Take Miller with you to help load the cubes."

Shooster looked at Houtt with a little contempt. He hated being told what to do. "I'll load them myself." He extended his middle finger and scratched the side of his head playfully. "Thank you very much."

"It's more of an accountability thing than a lifting thing. Buzz me when the drone arrives; I'll join you in bay, 3 it's a security issue." Houtt told him.

Miller was still splashing paint around his quarters when he glanced over to his monitor. He noticed the infrared image everyone thought was a person was no longer visible. He rang up Manetti." Hey Vince, take a look at your infrared."

He chuckled his familiar chuckle and said, "Well, I'll be, whatever or whoever it is must have died because it aint showin no signs of life now."

Lewis saw it too, and with some apprehension breathed a sigh of relief, at least for now.

Another digital message left the ship bound for Earth. Miller's communications system beeped as the message left. He just smiled knowing that whoever sent that message sent it out through everyone else's system too. Houtt was about to visit Lewis again when Shooster called.

"Hey you need to come down to the bay area and see this. Just when you think things can't get stranger."

Houtt appeared within the minute, but before he got to the bay area he had already felt the slight nudge and heard the bump of another ship docking. Judging by the depth of the thud, he knew this was no drone. He poked his head in the bay area and told Shooster to meet him at the air docks. Both men stood there watching the lights in air chamber 2 turn from red to green in series from outside the ship to inside. They could tell their new visitor was a woman, but who and why? Better question was, why was there no information given to anyone about this? This was a huge breach in protocol. The figure stood just outside the last of three doors waiting to enter the ship. Shooster stood on his toes and peeked in the small window. "I see no weapon." He hit the switch and opened the door. The woman entered, removed her helmet and introduced herself to Houtt and Shooster. She had strong attractive facial features, she wore no makeup and her hair was buzzed short. Somehow this look worked for her. Both men found her attractive not that that would matter because both men also knew this situation was no good.

She reached out her hand to Houtt first. "Lisa Lark," she said as she shook his hand.

Shooster stuck his hand out and introduced himself. "Rick Shooster they call me Shoe most of the time."

"Shooster is third in command on the ship." Houtt added.

"Nice to meet you gentlemen, I suppose you're wondering why I'm here, right?" She asked.

"Well things have not been the norm around here so to be honest nothing surprises us. But yeah we would like to know what's going on and who you work for."

"First, lets get these cubes loaded so I can send my crew back. Then I have a few things to discuss with you." She put her helmet back on and started to go back out when Houtt tapped her on the shoulder. She turned, removed her helmet and asked, "Yes?"

"You'll have to forgive me, but those cubes aren't going anywhere until I see some documentation or some orders or something. Things have been a little too weird around here for me to just let them go."

"Fair enough." She unzipped her spacesuit exposing just enough cleavage to validate she was a woman, pulled out a sealed envelope and handed it to Houtt. He broke the seal, slid some papers from the envelope, read them, slid them back in then handed them back to Lisa. "We'll load them on this side and your crew can unload them on your side." He turned to face Shoe. "Looks like she's staying with us all the way to Gate 6."

"Just great," Shooster mumbled.

Two hours later Lisa was standing back inside Quincy 4 asking Houtt if he could assemble the men and meet her on the bridge.

All five men sat in their perspective seats, leaving Lisa to find a seat on the small set of steps leading down to the bridge. "Gentlemen, my name is Lisa Lark and I have been sent here by The Three Day Shuttle Company. The reason I am here, is because your plans have changed. You are now on a fast track to C-Gate 6. What was planned as a routine dump is now anything but routine. As you are all aware by now the ships memory and the guidance cubes have been removed and confiscated." She was interrupted by Miller.

"Confiscated?" He asked looking around the room at his fellow travelers. He was met by shrugs and blank stares. "Why were they confiscated? We just figured they were being put to better use."

"I wish I had an answer for you fellas but I don't. All I know is, I was escorted out here by authorities of the shuttle company. Another thing I know is, we had to track you by honing in on those cubes. None of our other methods of contact and communication seemed to work. When was the last time someone ran a security check on your remaining systems? Your ship looks like it's docked at Gate 3 getting components removed which was the original plan. If anyone was to check your whereabouts that's where they would think you are. Regardless of the fact C-Gate 3 is now weeks behind us. So, in a sense, this is a ghost ship and the only thing to stop you at Gate 6 is the remaining cube, which still has the redundant safety stop on it. Once we get to Gate 6, it will be our job to bring everyone left there operating the Gate back home. Or in our case, back to Gate 4 where they will be reassigned. Total number of extra passengers will be seven. We'll have spare sleeping quarters for four. This means we ask them to double up. Each of you and myself included will be assigned new quarters for our journey back. Once we send Quincy 4 past Gate 6 we'll board the work ship The Drake and make our way back. Any questions?"

"Can we back up to where you said we're now on a fast track to Gate 6? What does that mean for us?" Lewis questioned.

"That means we're nonstop to Gate 6. This should reduce our time by a good forty percent considering we will no longer have to decelerate to make port entries. We now have authority to set engines at ninety percent."

Lewis' face turned white as a sheet. He just sealed his fate. He was supposed to get off at Gate 4 with Manetti and make his way back to Earth disguised as a laborer. Since Gate 4 was scratched both men were expecting to disembark at Gate 5 instead.

"I have a concern," Manetti said.

"You are?" Lisa queried.

"Vince Manetti. I'm scheduled for retirement. Made my decision to get off this boat at Gate 4, surrender my bonus and go home. I have resolved myself to exit at Gate 5 now. And you're telling me, I'm not getting off at all?"

"I wish I had better words for you Mr. Manetti but sadly I don't. Everyone on board is under the same contract with new job descriptions. I'm sorry to be the one who had to tell you this. Anyone else?" Miller took a step forward.

"Did I hear you correctly? You had to hone in on our cubes to find us? And everyone thinks we're docked at Gate 3? We never even docked there to begin with."

"All I know at this point is... this vessel appears to be docked at Gate 3. There is no communications left on board. Memory has been A.M.P.'ed and I was sent here to try to figure out why. "She turned to Houtt. "Mr. Houtt, set speed at ninety percent and let's get us and Mr. Manetti home before the sunsets."

The slight increase in the whirr of the engines was almost inaudible on the ship, but in the barge that was a different story.

Kester Trewer was now two days into cold turkey withdrawals from his dope. He lay under the old couch he found. The cushions now soaked with sweat and urine. Uncontrollably shaking with cold sweats and dry heaves. He was curled up in the fetal position again and every time a spasm shot through his body it would bring his knees up to his face in pain. To make matters worse, a fever from infection started and his body was drained of all energy. Dressed only in his underwear, he screamed and cried for help into the cold black abyss of rotting garbage. He had enough senses left to understand he just heard the tug's engines increase. This was it, he knew now his end was going to be when the barge imploded from the heat of the sun. Another spasm shot through his body so fierce his bowels let go. He thought for sure only blood squirted out but judging by the smell, he knew he didn't even have his underwear left.

Chapter 6

C-Gate 4

"At this speed we'll reach Gate 6 in under sixty days" Shooster said to anyone who was listening.

Houtt and Manetti already knew that reaching C-Gate 6 was the last of their worries. Things went from bad to worse since the arrival of Lisa Lark, who claimed to be a P.R. woman from the shuttle company.

"Something is terribly wrong." Houtt said.

Both Manetti and Shooster turned towards him.

"We have no memory, we have no guidance system to speak of and our footprint has us docked at Gate 3. We had something we thought was a person living in the garbage and now we have a representative from our company on board. What is going on?"

Shooster spoke up. "Well whatever you do, don't plug up anymore toilets. With the cubes gone we have nothing left to hold up the pipes for Lewis."

The other two men slowly turned their heads and looked at Shoe. "What? What did I do?" He said.

"Say that again," Houtt asked.

"I said don't plug up anymore toilets. With the cubes gone there is nothing left on board to hold up the pipes for Lewis."

"What pipes?" Manetti asked.

"Lewis took apart the auxiliary pump lines when he went to fix that plugged toilet. He told me he found it leaking and he had to disassemble it from the start to reach the leak. He called me and asked if I would hold the pipes up so he could band them back together. I suggested he use one of the cubes since it was about the same height he needed. So he went up to bay 3 and grabbed one."

Houtt raised his voice and asked. "He did what?"

"I didn't see any harm, I mean they were scheduled to be picked up and they were just sitting there. I sure wasn't gonna stand there for hours holding up pipes for him. He put it back. I watched him." Shooster said in an apologetic voice.

Houtt and Manetti scampered out and headed for Lewis's quarters. Neither man bothered to knock or buzz, they just forced their way in. Without saying a word Manetti had him backed into the wall with his feet off the floor. "What's going on?" He demanded.

Lewis could only smile. Houtt walked up next to Manetti and repeated the question. "What's going on?"

"It doesn't matter anymore, we're all dead." He laughed in Manetti's face. "Now put me down."

"Start talking and start talking now!" Houtt retorted.

"I set you guys up, all four of you were supposed to go right past Gate 6. I couldn't take the chance of any of you returning with stories of strange things happening on this mission." He turned back to Vince and said. "You and I were supposed to get off at Gate 4, only it was going to be just me. I had already requested orders be waiting there for you. Either finish the mission as contracted or face four years on the rails and lose your pension. You would have been forced to stay on board and meet the same fate as the others. Only something went seriously wrong and I was double crossed. Governor Trewer this time made sure I would never again be part of his life."

"What does Governor Trewer have to do with this mission?" Manetti asked.

"Remember during the last summit on Earth when that garbage barge was blown up?"

"Go on." Manetti ordered.

Houtt was pacing the floor. The more Lewis spoke the more he knew there was no good end to this story.

"That was me. I sent four idiots over the wall to place the charges. I lied to em about the launch schedule. When the smoke cleared they found six bodies not four. I was just as surprised as the guys who put the other two bodies in there. I was arrested on the scene and quickly hauled away and sentenced to four years as Yoman on the rails. Governor Trewer and Canadian Prime Minister Wells were responsible for the additional bodies. I was the only other person in the world who knew the count of six bodies was the truth. The only news reporter who reported six bodies was accidentally tossed down a flight of stairs and died. Trewer and Wells decided I was worth more alive than dead. At least, up until this point anyway, so, basically I got a free pass."

"Ok so what's going on with this ship? Houtt asked.

By now Miller, Shooster and Lisa were all listening in on the conversation.

"I Hackjacked the ship just before Gate 3. I switched our identity for the derelict ship The Sandra K. So anyone looking for us will think we stayed an extra day or two at Gate 3 and The Sandra K. is on her way to the Sun to be scuttled. So far the plan worked."

Shooster spoke up. "We still have our redundant failsafe. I installed it myself. I crossed every terminal on all six of those cubes until I found it."

"Correction," said Lewis. "I changed it out. I deliberately took the pump apart and hinted to you," he nodded at Shooster. "I hinted to you I needed something about the size of a cube or I needed you to hold the pipes for me. I knew you wouldn't hold the pipes, it was just like playing with a stacked deck, you bought it."

The seconds that followed that statement found Frank Lewis picking himself up from the floor and wiping the blood from his lip. Shooster went after him again but was stopped by Miller and Manetti.

"Come with me Lewis." Houtt ordered. You're under house arrest."

Lewis busted out laughing. "House arrest?! Have at it man. We're all going to fry. Burn baby burn. Lock me up. Shoot me. Torture me, I don't care anymore. I'm in this mess just like the rest of you."

"You made the mess." Miller reminded him.

"Boy don't I just feel stupid!" Lewis spat blood on the floor and offered his hands to Houtt in a mockery of wearing hand cuffs.

With Lewis sequestered in his room everyone else gathered on the main bridge and started frantically running systems checks on every system they could. Lisa took Lewis's seat and started running through the plumbing systems to see if there was anything they could use as far as software was concerned.

Houtt started in on the communications systems. There wasn't much in the way of stored information, in fact there was none. Everything was either surrendered near Gate 3 with the rendezvous ship or it was dumped at A.M.P. He did, however, have the ship's log. The ship's log was on an independent computer loop *and* hand written in his log book. He studied the patterns of the doors and hatches trying to map out where Lewis started and finished. He checked which hatches and doors were opened and closed and at what times. Miller started in on equipment systems. He checked the escape pods to see if they could be activated. No luck. He figured the cube that operated the pods was confiscated. None the less he powered each of the six escape pods up. First he powered them collectively. He got nothing, Then he powered each one separately. Again he got nothing. He tried powering pods two, four and six. He got nothing. He tried pods one, three and five. He still got nothing. He checked them all again. Now every one's biggest fear came true. Those pods died when their cube was removed.

Manetti took half the communications systems and started running checks to see if there was anything overlooked. An antenna that could be adjusted or a communicator on a different frequency but all he could manage at this stage was to broadcast his profanity throughout the ship.

Shooster was in charge of the barge. Not much help there he thought; however, he continued to run systems checks. Still pumping oxygen in the barge to filter it, all the check valves were working up to specs. He turned on the infrared scan again. He could see the small blotches of reddish orange light everyone thought were rats. In contrast to the volume of the barge, they appeared to be pin pricks. He figured they must have a life sustaining area because even though he could make them out scurrying about, they didn't travel far. No sign of the larger image, it must have died.

Kester sat up checking his surroundings. He had no clue where he was, what time of day it was or what day of the week it was. All he knew was, detox was over and for the first time in twenty years he was drug free.

The pain in his leg was excruciating. He cupped both his hands around his leg and ran them from his knee to his ankle. There was a large hump in his shin bone where the leg had set wrong. At this point, there was no sense in trying to reset it. Next he noticed the gaping hole in his chest that started out as two button size burns. His flesh was rotten and the smell was enough to make him gag. On one hand he wished he could see how bad it was; on the other hand he was glad he couldn't. He took his nasty underwear and brushed himself off, being careful not to smear his open wound. There was no way his injured leg would support him. He stood up on his good leg, fumbled in the dark for something he could use as a splint. He tore open the couch that had been his shelter, ripping the material into strips. He wrapped his leg tight. *"Without re-breaking it and re-setting it, this was as good as it was going to get."* The voice in his head told him he was gonna die anyhow. Even though it could be weeks, possibly months he could still be alive. He rolled the sofa on to its back exposing the bottom. He could feel springs and material but nothing else. He wondered what was above him and what was below him, after all he was in a barge the size of a small state almost, and surely it can't be a huge task to find something to make a splint from.

He heard movement. To his disbelief he heard it again. At first he thought it was the garbage shifting around him but it was getting closer. What he heard was not like a rustle of an animal it was more like a slicing sound. A swooshing sound. It sounded like paper being scooted across the floor. As it got closer the sound began to slow down. He was not alone. He began to panic just a little. He found his way to behind the couch. He crouched making himself as small as possible when he felt the head of the snake first. It slithered over his back. He couldn't tell what kind of snake it was. Snakes in the dump were quite common place he remembered. Where there was garbage there was a food source for rats which in turn became a food source for snakes. He laid still even after the tail of the snake slithered over his back and left his little sofa cave. "There must be rats close by," he said in a low whisper. "That means there is more food close by, too." Kester had a whole new notion of what food was and he became willing to eat what he could keep down in order to survive.

"How ironic," he thought. *"I'm fighting to stay alive only to die in the Sun's heat."*

Lisa said, "I got nothing. I don't see anything where plumbing is going to be our answer for a communication line."

Houtt reminded her that everything on the ship was run from a central command computer.

"Oh you mean the computer that has no memory or maybe the computer that has had its memory AMP'ed? In either case I still can't see where plumbing is our answer."

Houtt also reminded her that it was Lewis who was the ships plumber. So if there is a way off this ship that he knows of, it will be hidden in the plumbing system somewhere. She decided to recheck all the systems again, this time backwards.

Houtt was going through the log book, sentence by sentence, looking for anything that could be of some use.
"Maybe he's telling us the truth." Maybe there is no way off this ship and no way to stop it at Gate 6. Maybe there is no way to get a message out or get a message in anymore."

Shooster spoke up. "Lewis got both, messages in and messages out. All on his personal devices and all digital remember?"

"And all in code," Houtt added. "Maybe I should go see how he's doing."

Lewis was laying on his bed staring at the ceiling when Houtt walked in. "Knew you'd be back," he said. "You have questions you think I have answers for right?"

Houtt acknowledged with a nod of his head.

"Look man I got nothing. If I had anything, I would tell you. I would rather face the unknown kangaroo court than die out here like this. I have no back up plan and I have no escape plan. This was carefully orchestrated months ago. It went wrong. I guess you could call it karma. I'm just as dead as you; just like Miller. Just like Manetti and Shoe, and just like what's her name who is here for whatever reason. If anyone has a way out of here it won't be me. It will be that woman. She showed up out of the blue on some public relations gig months away from Earth. She's your answer Jim, not me."

"What does Never On Wednesday mean?" Houtt asked.

"Yeah you see if it didn't go wrong for me, you would never had gotten that message. The numbers spelled out Never On Wednesday, take the first letter of each word."

"NOW" Houtt said. "So what does it mean, this NOW?"

"NOW was the time for the hackjack that's all."

"Ok then who sent it to you?"

"Wells sent it to me, this was his idea all along. Canadian Prime Minister Barry Wells is behind all of this, and I'll lay you odds the pretty lady is one of Wells lackeys. It seems she is expendable too."

Houtt raised up and said. "Yeah, well *I'm* not expendable and *I* will find a way off this ship. My family *will* see me again, this I promise you."

Houtt stormed out and went back to the bridge. He sat there looking down at his hands and couldn't believe what he just heard. He was running his fingers over the hand that had no finger nails left. Staring down, rubbing that hand …. He bolted up from his chair, grabbed his tools and darted off to the sublevels of the ship. Shooster and Miller followed. Manetti and Lisa, watched in wonderment but stayed on the bridge to continue to do systems checks.

Once Houtt made it to the communications panels, Shoe and Miller helped him open the covers. No one knew what he was doing and Houtt himself was not really sure. He remembered a series of relay switches from the day he got zapped down here. He wondered if there was a way to cross these over and at least get an S.O.S. out into space. Someone somewhere would pick it up and rebroadcast it to every receiver from Gate 4 back to Earth. They had nothing to lose at this point.

Kester came to, not knowing how long he'd been unconscious. Time no longer had a meaning to him in his current location. He stood up, as painful as it was at least he was standing on both legs. He hobbled to the edge of his little cavernous spot and started feeling his way through the garbage again. Any step up is a step in the right direction. He started by standing on the couch and feeling above him. Dirt and grime filtered down on his head and face. He blew and spit the debris away. He could hear the faint drip of water which led him to believe he was on the right path. He found a smooth surface to place a knee on and when he did he lifted himself up. *"Steady,"* he kept telling himself and from a kneeling position to standing position the dripping water became a little louder. Feeling in every direction he squeezed between two wooden panels. His chest dragging across one of them made him flinch with pain but he kept going. Past the wood were more pieces of furniture. He tested each one to see how firm and steady they were. Stepping up on what he thought was a chair he started to teeter and took a moment to secure his balance. Blindly ducking and weaving his way, progress was slow, inches at a time. He could now see just a tiny hint of red light. There were old cans and bottles lying around him to his left. He tried to get around them but found the path blocked. He shuffled his feet like an old man through the cans, he could feel his toes pressing down on the sharp ridges where the cans had been open. He shuffled his feet a few more times stopping when he hurt his big toe by kicking a full can. He bent down to pick it up and discovered several other unopened cans. Not being able to tell what was in them he tried to carry a can in each hand. When he came out the other side of the cans there were several pieces of old wood. The way they were dumped reminded him of a teepee. He removed one of the boards and started to place it around him trying to find an angle up. He then placed another board next to it and then another. He had absolutely no idea if this would hold him but he started to shinny up the boards. The further up he went, the warmer the air became and the more he could see the dim red light. In what seemed to be a several days journey he found himself back on top of the garbage. With his sights set on the dim red light he continued to make his way across the pile; gathering as he went, pieces of clothing and material to cover his body and to hold the unopened cans of food he was carrying in his hands.

Chapter 7

C-Gate 5

Governor Trewer and William were sitting in stopped traffic. "Must be an accident ahead," William suggested. He studied the Governor in the rear view mirror. He seemed to be a new man since the disappearance of his son. There was a peace about him, a new serenity if you will. The Governor never looked up from his paper work nor did he say a word to William about the traffic jam. He picked up the phone and called ahead to his office to let his receptionist know he would be running late.

"Hello, Governor Trewer's office, this is Sarah how may I help you?" The sweet voice on the other end said.

"Good morning Sarah, how are you?"

"Just fine sir, thank you, and yourself?"

"There seems to be a traffic jam and I'm running late."

"Yes sir Mr. Governor, I will inform all of your appointments today that you're under the weather and I wish you a speedy recovery. Perhaps you have the 24 hour bug my kids had last week. It's been going around you know?"

"Good old Sarah," Trewer thought. *"She always has my back."* He wanted to try to get a feel for whoever was waiting for him in the office.

"Is it personal or business?" He asked her.

"Yes sir, I understand and personally if it were me, I would just stay in bed too." She answered.

"Civilian or government?"

"If it's really something that can't wait until you feel better I can send a copy of that action to your home computer. The Government Center is no place for you to be."

"Local?"

"Yes sir."

"Police department or Mayor's office?"

"I'll put that agenda item first on your list to inspect tomorrow morning. Yes sir, I have all your appointments in front of me. You get some rest and I hope to see you in the morning... Sir? "

"Yes?" He answered with a wry grin on his face, knowing what was coming next.

"Since your office will be closed for the day, I'll just take my work home and spend the day with my kids if you don't mind."

"Not at all Sarah, enjoy your day, you just earned it. Good bye and thanks again." He hung up his phone, then instructed William to turn around. "When we get back home you can take the rest of the day off, my treat."

Sarah hung up the phone in the Governor's office, looked up at inspector Martin Smith. "I'm sorry Inspector, the Governor will not be in today, and he seems to have a touch of the flu." She straightened the stack of papers on her desk, stood up, picked up her purse then gave a stinging smile to the Inspector. "Might I suggest an appointment next time, our Governor is a very busy man and your chances of seeing him will be much greater with an appointment. Good day Inspector." She stood at the door holding it open.

"And a good day to you as well, and I trust Governor Trewer is probably feeling a bit better as we speak." The inspector took a quick glance around the receptionist office and walked out.

Back at the Governor's home William parked the car, bid the Governor a good day then retired to his modest home that sits on the back of the grounds. Governor Trewer sat down on his big plush sofa trying to figure out what course of action to take on this latest development. His phone rang.

"Hello?" he answered without first looking to see who was calling.

"Governor Trewer so good to hear your voice this morning," a chirpy man's voice said.

"Who am I speaking with?" Trewer asked.

"This is Inspector Martin Smith. You may remember me from the rail disaster of a few years ago. I was put in charge of that investigation, at least I was in charge until I was pulled off and given a desk job for two years. Funny thing about a desk job though, it gives you so much more time to think about things..."

He was interrupted by Trewer. "Inspector that case has been closed for a long time, I'm afraid I have nothing more to offer you."

"Yes I am aware that that case is closed, I'm calling on another matter this morning."

"Then how can I help you inspector and please keep in mind I am a very busy man and my time is in high demand."

"Yes sir. I understand you had a full schedule this morning that is until you came down with that nasty flu bug your receptionist told me about. I'll be brief sir, since Detective Miles was pulled off the investigation of the bloody mystery that took place in your home and the subsequent disappearance of your son Kester... well, I just called you to let you know I'm now in charge of the investigation. I want to thank you in advance for your future cooperation and I look forward to helping you out in your time of need. You must be devastated not knowing the whereabouts or the fate of your only son."

"I have my sleepless nights Inspector, thanks for calling but as you already know I should be taking it easy today. Goodbye." Trewer did not even wait for the inspector to say goodbye before he hung up.

Lisa lowered her head phones and spoke softly but direct. "Your life force seems to have resurfaced."

Shooster and Miller were still running system checks looking for anything that would help them now. Houtt was still in the lower decks trying to rewire the short distance communications antenna. Manetti was in his quarters typing a journal of the past few month's records. Not knowing if they would ever be read; nonetheless it gave him something to do.

Lisa's voice came over the intercom system. "Gentlemen, your life source just resurfaced."

Manetti turned his personal screen on to take a look. Houtt laid down his tools and rode the elevator up to the main deck. Lewis sprang up like a shot from a gun, leapt across his bunk and turned his personal screen on too. He stood there with his jaw open in disbelief. *"How could anyone or anything for that matter survive months in a garbage barge in deep space? This is impossible,"* he thought. Lewis wanted out of his room and started to buzz for someone to open his door.

Lisa just sat there and stared at the large monitor on the control deck. "Whatever that is, it's making its way to the connection wall. Very slowly I might add."

Miller leaned in for a closer look and muttered. "What do you think the temperature is in there? I mean it must be warm enough to sustain life. We've been months in space now and this thing is still alive? What do you 'spose it is?"

"Heat from the main engine discharge blowers run through that part of the barge and I'm sure there is or was enough rotting food to keep something alive but I'm with you Miller...what is it?" Shooster chimed in.

Houtt made it to the control deck, removed his glasses and simply whispered "what the?" "Then he turned towards a blinking red light. "How long has Lewis been buzzing us?"

Lisa answered. "Started right after I called everyone on the intercom."

"He knows something and if he knows something that means what we're looking at is another human being."

Shooster just laughed.

"Unfreakingimpossible," Miller added.

"What else can it be?" said Houtt, as he turned towards Miller and Shooster.

"I'm going to have to have another word with our plumber it seems. Never did trust that sad excuse of a man and I've questioned his presence since his arrival. He was a scum bag back in the day and he's still a scum bag now. And I swear on my mothers remembrance if Lewis knows anything about this I'll send his sorry butt straight to the vacuum of space and not think twice." He started to walk from the command deck when Lisa stood up and placed her hand on his chest.

"Stand down Mr. Houtt." She told him with a cold steel look on her face.

"Excuse me?!"

"I said stand down, no one on this ship is going to have any more contact with Francis Lewis." At that point she removed a small black cloth from her personal carrying case. She carefully unrolled the package to reveal a hand gun in a holster and an I.D. wallet with her picture on one inside flap and a silver badge on the other.

"I'm in charge of this mission now, my direct orders are to monitor the crew and look for Kester Trewer as a stowaway. Since no one on board is dead yet, and until I am, you will do what I ask when I ask. Is that understood gentlemen?"

Her lips curled up in some grotesque smile that all of a sudden made her more unattractive than any unshowered and unshaved man on board.

"Hold on just a minute. You expect us to just believe this?" Miller asked in a loud voice.

"Wish I could make this easier for you boys; however, with all outside communications cut off, I have no way to confirm the situation. Please take your seat Mr. Houtt and you as well Mr. Miller." She opened the intercom system and paged Manetti to the control deck.

"As soon as Mr. Manetti arrives, I'll tell you what I know and give you information on what's to be expected."

Ten minutes later Manetti walked up and sat down in his chair.

"What's going on now?" He asked.

Lisa positioned herself in front of all four men.

"Gentlemen, my name is Lisa Lark. I'm a Captain with the Federal Commission of Universal Law Enforcement. The FCULE placed me on board this ship to look for a stowaway who goes by the name of Kester Trewer, yes guys that's Trewer as in Governor Trewer. The Governor's son went missing within twenty four hours of the beginning of this mission. We currently have other agents scouring Gates 2, 3 and 4 which is why we won't be stopping until we reach Gate 6. Everything you men did was to prepare for my arrival. Some of it was planned and some of it was just pure dumb luck. Unfortunately I suspect, we found our man in the barge." She nodded towards the infra-red image on the large screen. "Regardless, I've been instructed to search the ship and the four of you will help me."

Manetti stood "I'm not searching squat lady. You still think we're getting off this coffin at Gate 6, don't you? You sat right here and listened to all that crap about being Hackjacked and about our A.M.P. being ordered weeks in advance." He raised his voice and took three steps in Lisa's direction which prompted both Miller and Houtt to stand up to defend her.

"We're dead, we're a ghost ship for crying out loud. They think we're still docked at Gate 3 don't you get it?" Manetti continued.

She in turn, took two steps forward, placed her face inches from Manetti's, dropped her arms to her sides and standing toe to toe with the infuriated bald man and yelled back at him.

"Listen old man, in case you haven't noticed? I'm on the same death ride as the rest of you. Our only chance to get off this coffin as you so eloquently put it is to find Kester Trewer alive on board this boat. Then, maybe then someone will take notice and figure out how to reach us. We have nothing but time on our hands but let me say this...The more time we spend fluffing up our cock feathers the more time we lose to becoming London broil."

"We don't stand a chance lady, have you not paid any attention to what's really going on?"

Manetti was dangerously close to becoming physical when Houtt stepped up to the conversation.

"Easy man, you're not the only one here who's afraid. We all are, and we need to do what we can to see we get off this thing."

Manetti turned and pushed Houtt backwards, luckily he landed in his seat unharmed.

"Aint gonna happen Jim, you understand this right? It aint gonna happen. We're gonna fry, we're gonna be baked man." He shot an arm straight up like a Nazi salute. "To the Sun! You following me man? You picking up what I'm putting down man? You smellin what I'm sellin man?"

By now Houtt was back on his feet and placed a finger in Manetti's chest. He started to thump him one poke with each word.

"Don't (poke) you (poke) ever (poke) touch (poke) me (poke) again! Do I make myself clear?"

Manetti turned to walk away when Houtt grabbed him by the arm and spun him back around. "Don't walk away when I'm talking to you. I put up with your crap for far too long and I'm ready to end it right here and now."

The two men stood toe to toe both red faced and shaking waiting for the other to blink first.

"Floods." Shooster said quietly. "Floods," he repeated

"What you talking about Shoe?" Miller asked

"The flood lights inside the barge. They should work. If it's warm enough to see infra-red images then it should be warm enough to turn those flood lights on."

Houtt broke eye contact with Manetti and glanced at Shooster.

"Is this true?" Captain Lark asked.

Houtt shrugged his shoulders, "Don't know, we never had this situation before. If it is true we need to rewire the switches to see if we can turn them on."

"Well what are you waiting for?" she asked. "How long do you think this will take?"

"Two days if I have some help, a week if I work alone." Houtt answered.

"Take Manetti with you. While you're doing that the three of us will start looking on ship to see if he's a stowaway, even though I think our man is in the barge. Orders are orders and my orders are to search this ship. Shooster you take sub levels one through three, I'll take four and five and Miller you take this top deck. Keep communications open and report anything that looks like a person might have camped out on."

Shooster looked at Miller with that I got more seniority than you look, but reluctantly headed to the bottom of the ship.

Houtt turned to Manetti, "you done pushing me around now?"

"If you're done thumping me in the chest."

The two men joined Shoe and Captain Lark in the elevator and headed down.

Kester sat up and tried to judge the distance between him and the red light. He pondered why he was heading there to begin with. The infection on his chest caused his skin to start to rot and he needed to find a way to cover the wound. His eyes became accustom to the faint red light and he could make out more of his surroundings now that he was back to the top of the garbage.

He checked his immediate surroundings for anything he could use. Tearing open synthetic bag after synthetic bag in search for who knows what. He tore open a third bag and a horrible stench squelched out at him along with several maggots and other scavenger insects. He started to gag and spent the next fifteen minutes in dry heaves. By the time he was finished it felt like his eye balls were detached from their sockets. He looked down into his lap only to find maggots by the hundreds squirming around on his naked genitals and thighs He jerked himself up and began to swat and brush off the white larva. Picking through his pubic hair until every last maggot had been removed from his body. He looked inside the bag and knew if there was anything in his stomach he would have regurgitated it on the spot. In the bag were the carcasses of two small animals and one large one. He assumed they were dead pets probably cats or dogs. He pushed the bag to the side and inch by painful inch moved on to the next pile of synthetic bags. He estimated them to be about twenty five feet away which was also the distance he estimated to be the limit of his sight.

It took him almost five hours to traverse those twenty five feet and when he did finally reach the pile of bags he was a little more cautious about ripping them open. His fingers hurt from pulling his deteriorating body over and under the maze of garbage and debris. He allowed himself some time to rest and as hard as he tried, he could not shake the thought of all those maggots. He laid on his back panting and wringing his hands trying to get his fingers to cooperate with the brain. Suddenly there was a sensation on his chest. Too tired to even move his head he tried to ignore the feeling. He placed his left hand over his wound to try to judge the area of the sensation. Afraid to look, thinking he might find internal organs exposed he just lay there covering the gaping hole with his filthy hand.

"Why am I not dead?" he spoke to himself. "I've been living in a barge headed towards the sun for God only knows how long. I'm naked, I'm infected, I'm starving and yet I keep moving to that stupid red light like it has some significance in my life." He started to laugh out loud, he rolled his head back and opened his mouth to the top of the barge and hysterically laughed.

"I'm going insane," he cried at the top of his lungs between laughs. "Completely crazy," he continued.

"Hey Kester!" he shouted to himself. "You forget to mention covered in maggots," again laughing hysterically. For almost two minutes he had forgotten where he was and what his fate was going to be. He laid on his back breathing heavy with tears washing streaks of clean face running down to his neck.

"You forgot covered in maggots.... you forgot covered in maggots" he was now exhausted and whispering ... you forgot covered in mag... He drifted off into a comatose deep sleep.

2 days later

Houtt and Manetti were sitting in their command chairs on the bridge drinking coffee and watching the infra-red image on the screen. Miller walked in and sat down.

"Whatever it is, it's still alive but hasn't moved from that spot in almost forty eight hours. It moved about twenty feet or so a few days back. Took it about a day to do it too, but after that, right where you see it is right where it's been. How did you guys make out with wiring the flood lights?"

"They're wired and plugged in," Houtt answered. "Only thing now is to wait for miss prissy fit to give the order to turn them on. By the way where is she?"

Miller turned his chair sideways to look at both men. "She and Shoe have been making a prison cell for Frank." Miller chuckled.

"A prison cell?" Manetti chimed in.

"Yeah she got some bug up her butt about a safe place for Lewis so he couldn't hurt himself and she could keep him on ice until this mess is over," said Miller.

Manetti turned to Houtt. "She still thinks were getting off this tub doesn't she?"

"Maybe she knows something we don't," Houtt answered.

Miller pointed to the screen. "It's moving again only this time it's going backwards."

Chapter 8

Where's Kester ?

(Three weeks earlier)

"I'm not leading with this story anymore, I'm not leading with Kester Trewer, I'm not leading with the protests and I'm not leading with Governor Trewer. This is an old story and this network has whipped this dead horse long enough. Let those other losers continue to speculate on what happened. This story remains a dead story for this network until we have new information." Paul Downing spoke louder than usual as he slammed a stack of investigating folders on the polished oak table top in his press room.

"This is where you three come in." He glanced up at the three investigative reporters who were summoned to the press room.

"There's a story here." He waved his hand over the stack of folders which now resembled a splashed poker chip pot.

Millie Fisher and Buck Whistler were both seasoned investigating reporters with GBC and the arrival of Franz Hummel who defected from a competitive broadcasting company made them the perfect team.

"I got this Chief." Millie said as she stood up and walked to his end of the table to collect the folders. Millie was an attractive woman. Strong facial features, raven black hair and legs that would hypnotize a stone statue. She shuffled the folders back into a neat stack, then walked back around the table handing a few folders to Franz, a few folders to Buck and keeping a few for herself. Before she sat down she made eye contact with Paul.

"We'll scour the story and see what we can find, but you realize our ratings will suffer if we lose our audience because we abandoned this story." She smoothed her skirt under her legs as she sat back down to open her first folder.

"I know Millie, but honestly, there's nothing left of this story besides Governor Trewer has all the press locked out. No one gets close to anyone involved, directly or indirectly. I personally don't give a rat's patootie if we do nothing but fluff pieces for the next year, we are not revisiting this story without something new." Paul Downing stood to leave the room. "You're the best people I got, I want you to report to me every morning anything you find however big or however small ok?"

Millie answered first. "Yes Chief."

The other two men just nodded with confident smiles and watched their director walk out the door.

"Ok boys," Millie said as she stood up. "We'll meet at Drago's for lunch in three hours. In the meantime start going through these files and see what we missed."

The two men stood up as she sashayed out the door. Franz being the last man to leave the room turned the lights off and headed to his office. He had deep political informants on his list of people who owed him a favor and figured now is as good a time as any to start making phone calls.

William Moss's personal phone started to vibrate in his pocket. He ignored it and continued driving south. He'd been with the Governor long enough to know that somehow his boss knew something he wasn't going to tell. He decided to distance himself as far as he could for a while and get some well needed rest and relaxation. He took his vacation time and headed towards the family's private beach house where he was to meet up with his steady lady friend of five years.

Mi Su Lin was the beautiful daughter of Chinese immigrants who settled down in the opium den area of China Town. She met him at the door wearing only an opened short dark blue silk robe. Her body was perfect in every way. She kissed him on the lips and led him to a circle of pillows on the floor. Standing in front of him she slid her robe over her shoulders and let it float to the floor. His phone started to vibrate once again. Mi looked at him with that "*you better not answer that*" look on her face then stomped her foot on the floor and left the room when he did.

"What's up Franz, this better be good because a naked Chinese lady just stormed out of the room when I took this call. What you got for me?"

"Hey Bill, um, I don't have anything for you, matter of fact I was hoping I could ask you the same question. Bill, we got nothing on this Kester story man, and my editor and my director are scrambling for anything new we can use. I know you...." Franz's sentence was cut short by a now irate, screaming William Moss.

"What!" Moss yelled. "You did not just call me and expect me to have information for you? I knew I shouldn't have answered my phone. You trying to get me killed or are you just plain stupid?"

Franz tried to get a word in edgewise but gave up. His only real inside contact now was almost a total loss.

"I was beat, kicked and my car was spray painted green looking for Kester and what did you do?" He bellowed through snarled teeth. "Oh wait, let me guess. You sat on your fat butt and waited for someone else to do the dirty work. He aint on the planet anymore if you really want to know what I think. I got an idea, why don't *you* go looking for him in the recesses and cesspools of the underworld and report back to me? Or.... Better yet, grab a shuttle and comb the gates. He aint anywhere on this planet. Period. Get it? Got it? Good! Now leave me alone or I'll see to it you'll be reporting on the sunflower domes in Antarctica!

Franz did not become a seasoned investigative reporter by cowering every time someone raised their voice or threatened him and he wasn't about to back down now.

"Listen Bill you owe me and I'm calling my marker due. This story has a secret and I want it. Sunflowers or no sunflowers give me something I can take back to my boss. You have my word your name stays out of it. Unless....." He spoke slowly and clearly. "Unless you would prefer I go on record and say how irate you got when answering questions about the involvement of Governor Trewer in the disappearance of his own son?"

"I didn't answer any questions." Moss spoke with an exasperated exhale.

"Legally you did, Bill. You might not have given me the answers I want but you never said no comment, and by law, I can dissect and take out of context any number of the words in your answer. For example the phrase *Kester is not on this planet* will go a long way in the media, especially when it was quoted by the Governor's own staff."

William Moss' face just turned bright red with rage, he was pacing around the parameter of the circle of pillows.

"Honestly Franz, I got nothing I can go on record with, they're watching me and most likely listening to me too. You forget I'm still a person of interest in the investigation and anything I tell you can be construed as contempt of court or tampering with evidence or whatever other charges they want to slap me with. Don't think for one moment I won't get tossed under the bus just to put closure on this."

"Ok Bill you said you can't go on record, what about off the record?" The reporter asked with a hopeful tone in his voice.

"Seriously Franz? You're going to get me killed but here goes. Off the record right?"

"Off the record." Franz assured him.

"Off the record, The Governor knows something. I wouldn't say his demeanor has been somewhat joyous but it's not like a man who is worried about his son and it's really been creeping me out. Now if you don't mind I have a ticked off naked woman here, an opium pipe and a long needed vacation to get started, which by the way is still off the record."

"Still off the record Bill, enjoy your vacation and easy does it with the opium."

Franz ended the call which he recorded even though he knew since he never informed Moss it was being recorded it was all off the record to begin with. Placed his feet up on his desk top and started to run the conversation through his head.

William Moss stood in the doorway to the bedroom where Mi Su Lin was stretched out naked on his bed. He was now completely naked too with an opium pipe in his hand. She smiled at him and he returned the smiled. "Let the fun begin," he whispered.

The three reporters met at Drago's and took up space in a far corner of the restaurant, ordered drinks and asked the waitress to return in half an hour with menus.

"Ok Franz," Millie said with a hopeful tone in her voice. "What did Bill give you?"

"I got absolutely nothing I can use, and I mean nothing." He answered bitterly.

"Bill is a good source for us to keep in our corner and the last thing I need or want is to have his blood on the pages of this story."

"You call yourself a reporter!?" Millie squelched loud enough to turn a few heads. "This is big and you're concerned over the safety of your source?!"

"Now just hold on Millie, you know the game. You been playing it just as long as I have. Number one, who do you think Bill will call when it comes time to talk? And secondly, Bill, instead of suggesting I cram this story up my whazoo, suggested in a roundabout way I hop on a transport and go see for myself if Kester is aboard Quincy 4 while it's still holed up at Gate 3. Seems to me if I remember correctly, our company has deployed several drones throughout the entire recreational and commercial travel systems. So now I ask this question. Why don't we have one of those drones tailing that barge in the first place? And this brings me to a bigger question. Where is the nearest drone and how soon can we have one in the area?"

Buck opened his case and started typing on a small keyboard. Millie and Franz began perusing the menu the waitress had just dropped off while they waited.

"Looks like we have seven drones within thirty six hours from Gate 3. But I'm with you Franz, why is no one covering this story if not for any other reason than a fluff piece?"

Millie placed her menu down on the table and took out her phone. She pushed a single button on her phone and waited for her director to answer.

"Hello Paul. Hey listen we're sitting here wondering why no broadcasting companies are even covering this Quincy story. I mean if nothing else it could be used as fluff or filler right?" She laid the phone on the table and put it on speaker. "I have you on speaker Paul, so all three of us can hear."

"Well I certainly can't speak for any company but ours. It's my understanding, we have several camera drones as we speak, heading to Gate 4 to pick up the story. We have a solar filtered million pixel, ten thousand power telescopic drone waiting at Gate 6 to record back the implosion. Other than that, I guess no one has bothered to even consider it a story. Personally I think this is a waste of good time and broadcasting money but hey, at the end of the day, I'm just like you guys... I only work here."

"Thanks Paul" she hung up and sat there in silence with her two comrades waiting for the waitress to return so they could order lunch.

Buck closed his case, smiled and said. "There, I just rerouted drones 27, 134 and 57 to Gate 3 and the surrounding vicinity. We should have visual confirmation on Quincy within thirty six hours. So in the meantime we have a day and a half to structure this story and get the jump on everyone else. I'll let Paul know what's going on and the three of us will meet in the studio this time tomorrow with the story."

They enjoyed their lunch as best they could considering the three of them now had their noses crammed inside personal computers.

Lisa sat alone on the bridge. The dim blue lights from the control panels softly reflected the image of a woman who was scared to death but unable to show it to the rest of the crew. She watched as the infrared image now tried to move farther away from the red light. This cast even a greater shadow of doubt on whether or not she was really looking at a human being let alone her guy, Kester Trewer.

"Ok let's see what we got." She whispered to herself as she reached over and hit the toggle switch. A low hum could be heard coming from the control panel as the ballasts started to heat up eventually turning the flood lights on inside the barge. By the time she was joined on the bridge by Miller and Houtt, the first flicker of light was starting to bounce off the objects in the garbage. By the time Shooster and Manetti made their way to the bridge the entire barge was lit up like daylight. Houtt took a little pride in the fact his rewire job worked. Lisa called for the camera controls.

She began panning the camera back and forth starting as close to the red light as possible. Slowly they were looking at the debris. Discarded containers, old plastic chemical barrels by the hundreds, furniture, busted toys, electronics, and lead containers skewed sideways with the words nuclear waste stenciled on them in red paint. On the far wall stuck in a crevice with its hooves in the air was a dead horse. They could see the skin and flesh had been rotting off for quite some time. She panned in closer to the exposed underbelly of the animal.
"Really?" Shooster asked. "You think we want to see that?"

"Perfect source of food if you ask me and by the looks of things someone or something has dined here." She mumbled in a low soft tone.

She started to pan the camera back to the close side when Manetti excitedly said "There!"

She stopped.

"Where? What did you see?"

Manetti placed his finger on the large screen and repeated. "There."

"I don't see a thing." Houtt added and Miller agreed.

"What are you looking at Mr. Manetti?" Lisa asked.

"That right there, I used to have a game console just like that when I was a kid, spent hours distracting myself from life and homework playing those games." He chuckled.

"Lets be serious here." The woman officer said with a slight demand for order in her voice then continued to pan the camera. Slowly she sectored off the barge going inch by inch. She then zoomed in on a snake. Tapped the screen and said. "Not uncommon on these barges to have unwanted pets tossed away but this is a bit over the top." The python was coiled up nesting on a pile of old clothing. "I would say we just found our source of life, don't you agree gentlemen?"

"Except one thing madam detective." Miller spoke up.

"What's that?"

"What you're looking at is a Python Sebae or more commonly known as the African Rock Python. Impressive in size when full grown and obviously this one is not. This is a cold blooded reptile, *not* a warm blooded mammal which means our infrared would not have picked it up as a hot life force. So sorry to burst your bubble but this is not the source of our image... however this might be." He strategically placed his finger on the screen. "Zoom your camera on this image." He requested.

Everyone on the bridge leaned closer to the big screen and before the camera even enlarged the image they all knew it was human.

"Lisa zoomed in on an image of a naked man laying sideways on a pile of old plastic containers.

"This has got to be our man," she whispered.

"He's seen better days, looks like to me." Shooster spoke up.

"He may have seen better days but his life ended years ago when he became hooked on dope." Manetti put his two cents worth in.

"Keep zooming in on his face, let's get a better look." Shooster said.

By the time the camera stopped zooming, there was no doubt it was Kester and when he blinked his eyes, there was no doubt he was still alive.

"Well I'll be." Lisa said. That's our boy in living color and yes the pun is intended."

She looked around the room and noticed Jim Houtt was missing and she knew exactly where he went and figured by the time she got there Frank Lewis would be dead. She wasted no time. She jumped to her feet unholstered her side arm and took off in a sprint towards her makeshift cell and hoped Houtt didn't murder Lewis before she got there.

Houtt had Lewis pinned to the back wall, there was blood spattered behind him and on the floor but Lewis was still alive. The detective calmly placed the barrel of her weapon against the back of Houtt's head and suggested he cease his actions immediately because his life was nowhere near as important as Lewis's was at this point.

Houtt furiously and reluctantly released Lewis. No words needed to be said, the looks in both men's eyes told the story.

Lewis smiled and said. "Guess I got friends in high places." Then projected a mixture of spit, snot and blood on to the floor and Houtt's foot. Before Lisa had time to even digest what just happened, Houtt placed both his thumbs under the right eye socket of Frank Lewis then dropped the man to the floor. Wiped his shoe clean on Franks shirt then left him screaming on the floor with his right eye dangling from its socket.

Lewis carefully slid his eye back into place while Lisa stood there watching without assisting him.

"Frank," she said kneeling down to be at his level. "Seems to me if I was going to do what you did I would have researched this ship a little better. This is a Quincy line of tugs. Redundancy was the key safety factor when these ships were built. Sure you have everything off line now but before this ship was Hackjacked it initiated the life support system in the barge.

How stinking ironic is it that the very man you sentenced to die in the garbage is the very man who's life you spared. If there was one word I can think of right now to describe you ... idiot would be that word. Now as long as we have life on board this rattle trap it is my job to keep your smelly hind end alive, and trust me on this, the only reason I stopped Jim is because my orders are to bring you home to testify. From there it's none of my business what happens to you."

Lewis stood up with a hand covering his eye and blood dripping from his face. "You call me the idiot?!" He raised his voice and repeated. "You call me the idiot? That's really rich you know. You're the idiot madam inspector if you think for one minute I'll ever testify. Think again because this ship is a ghost, a specter, a figment, it don't exist. Don't you get it lady? I screwed up and when I did, I screwed us *all* up. No one knows where we are and no one has a way of finding out. They think we're docked at Gate 3 on some stupid PR campaign, gettin drunk and eating little green sandwiches until our hearts content."

"I don't believe that for one minute Mr. Lewis. You seem to have forgotten I found this ship and we had two drones find you as well." She spun on her heel to walk away. When she turned the corner of the corridor and was just out of sight Lewis yelled after her.

"Hey inspector lady, ask yourself this question. Where did you start your investigation? I'm betting it was at Gates one or two wasn't it?"

She stopped, took a few steps backwards, and leaned her head back so she could see him. She never said a word she just looked at the bloody smile on his face and the way his one good eye looked like insanity warmed over.

With red spittle splattering out of his mouth he nodded his head real slow then said. "Yep that's right lady, you took off on your little journey before Gate 3, and no one even knows you're here."

Chapter 9

(Find me a way)

Lisa Lark Investigative Detective sat at the end of the large white table in the mess hall of Quincy 4 trying not to look like her life was ending. As she glanced from each man sitting there with her." I want him out of there," she said in a matter of fact mono tone.

"Who?" Houtt queried.

"Kester Trewer, I want him out of that garbage barge and I want him out of there before he dies. Do we have a way to communicate with him? Is there a way in? What are my options?"

"Your options is just that lady!" Manetti blurted out. "I'm guessing you don't quite understand that we're in here and he's out there. I don't see an option I have here, how about you Shoe? How about you Miller? How about you Jim?" He went around the room asking. Before anyone else had the chance to utter a word Lisa stood up.

"In case anyone here missed the memo I'll repeat it. I am in charge on this vessel, I will order you, I will dictate to you and I will force you to do whatever it takes to get *that* man out of *that* dumpster." She was thrusting her finger towards the garbage hauler. "I don't want to hear we can't do this. We have shafts and duct work carrying the stench of air in and out of this ship to that barge and vice versa. According to the manual I read this morning those shafts are three feet in circumference and we have a total of six, three for good air and three for bad air. So find me a way! Now…. which one of you is going in?"

She gave Jim Houtt the once over. "Not you, you're too fat." She started to circumvent the table. She looked at Manetti, "stand up." He did. "You'll fit and take Shooster with you. The two of you have five hours to study this blue print and figure out how you'll do this."

Just as Miller was thanking his lucky stars he wasn't going in she stopped and hovered just behind his shoulders. She placed a hand on his left shoulder and said. "And you Mr. Miller will be the tool man so you go with them."

His heart sank, he suffered from claustrophobia as a child and over the years it became so bad he can't even look at a fellow work mate crawling through a tunnel without causing him anxiety. Everyone knew this was a bad idea but both Shooster and Manetti expressed a warped sense of deviant satisfaction. They knew he would freak out if he had to go in the duct work and both men thought it was funny.

"Can't send Miller." Jim Houtt spoke without lifting his eyes from his coffee cup.

"Scuse me?" Lisa said.

"I said, you can't send Miller through the duct work." He finally lifted his head and looked at her.

"I can and will send whomever I please thank you very much.

Jim Houtt just calmly looked her in the eye and said, "nope you can't, you might think you're in charge here and maybe you are, I don't know for sure and quite frankly I don't give a flip if you are or not. If you send Miller in that duct work, he'll freak out due to his medical condition of claustrophobia and quite possibly injure himself or someone else in the process. Therefore you can't send him in." He pointed to a smaller computer screen with Miller's medical records prominently displayed for everyone to see. He pointed to a line on the report and said. "See right here, severe claustrophobia documented medical disability." He looked up over his shoulder at Ms. Lark then said, "Since I'm too fat, it looks like you're the tool man for this job now."

Smiles stretched across the faces of Manetti and Shooster. Miller however relieved that he was not going in, still felt weak in front of the other men.

Lisa Lark was lost for words. "I'll be on the bridge studying those ducts, call me when you're ready." As she briskly walked away, she knew they were laughing behind her back.

Miller took his seat at the main control panel on the bridge. His designated job now, was to keep an eye on Kester for whatever reason. Detective Lark, Manetti and Shooster re-appeared on the bridge a few hours later arguing.

"That duct work has a labyrinth of 8 two inch thick screens and two fans in each one, you're totally insane to even think about this let alone going through with it. Besides that, Kester has not even moved an inch since we turned those spots on. Has he Miller?" Manetti was almost at the top of his lungs and spewing spit from the excitement in his voice.

"Not an inch since I've been sitting here anyhow." Miller answered.

Lisa poked a finger in Manetti's chest. "Now you listen to me and you listen good. Dead or alive that body goes home with us. So the job just became harder, big deal. I would tell you my heart bleeds for you, but it doesn't."

Manetti calmly removed her finger from his chest. "Touch me one more time and you'll be on the floor looking up at my smiling face wondering how the heck you just ended up down there. Do you have any idea of what we have to do to reach that strung out punk of a daddy's boy? You're talking dragging torches through there as we go. Cut one screen then back out, drag the torches back into the next screen and repeat that process eight times. Not to mention disconnect and remove two double bladed tunnel fans too! Do you even know how much a double blade tunnel fan weighs?"

She was about to talk when Manetti interrupted her with the answer.

"It weighs four hundred pounds if it weighs an ounce."

The veins on his forehead and temples were bulging like they were about to explode. He stormed off the bridge and disappeared to his personal quarters. Detective Lark turned to focus on Shooster who simply held his hands up like he was being robbed. He had a don't look at me look on his face. He backed away from her and left the bridge too.

She turned to speak to Houtt who was already standing in anticipation.

"You can't do it," he calmly said.

"Just disconnect those fans and leave the rest to me." she bellowed.

By now even Houtt was getting upset with this woman who, uninvited, joined their little nightmare.

"I'm telling you, you can't disconnect those fans. It's suicide for us all if you do. Those fans are designed to supply a constant pressure on the barge. One blade turns this way." He pointed to his left. "And the other turns that way." Pointing to his right. "They're what we call equalizing fans. We got four of them in the duct work. One fan goes out no problem, the redundancy system kicks in and shuts them all off. Only problem with that is... we no longer have our redundancy system. You loaded it and removed it a few weeks ago."

She stopped him, ran her hands through her sweat streaked hair and let out a frustrated growl. "Ok then what will happen if we cut the power to one of those fans without our redundancy system?"

"The duct work will implode, but before it implodes the effect will be like a teeny tiny (he held his forefinger and thumb about a hair's breadth away from each other) itsy bitsy black hole which will cause everything not bolted down including us to be forced inside and crushed."

Her face turned to stone and her eyes to steel. "Find me a way!" Then she left the bridge leaving Houtt and Miller standing there in disbelief.

Millie Fisher opened the door to her apartment to let Buck Whistler and Franz Hummel enter. She prepared a few snacks and had some beer on ice in her kitchen sink. The two men walked to the smell of fresh potpourri, removed their shoes and took up space on her sofa. She already had the large wall screen turned on with a non-stop live image of Niagara Falls.

"Ok guys we're going to live feed from Gate 3 in seven minutes. We all know hacking into a drone is illegal even though every station does it. If you want to leave now, there's the door don't let it clip you in the heels on the way out." Her statement didn't phase either of her guests, who were now filling plates with finger foods and opening cold beer.

"Going to live feed in 3- 2 -1 and now we're live at Gate 3. This is drone 27 equipped with infrared imaging, deep ping capabilities and a stealth chip. I took the liberties of notifying the officials at Gate 3. I informed them we will have three drones mapping and collecting positioning data. To them this is just hassle news story that requires they be in proper position in accordance to orbital laws. Simply put guys, Gate 3 in the past had tendencies to drift outside its allotted coordinates. They think we're here checking up on them and no one will suspect otherwise. Oh yea, and by the way, I received word today through my sources that GNBC, OCBS and UABC are all waiting at Gate 4 for Quincy 4 to show up. Matter of fact Stony O'Donnell from GNBC asked me to let him know when the ship departs Gate 3. I told him no problem." She chuckled along with her two workmates.

"What are we looking at now?" Buck asked.

"That my friend is a waste barge, by comparison to barge one would be like placing a raisin next to a watermelon. This is all human waste and judging by its location I would say it's getting ready to launch." No sooner had Franz said that, a green light came on and a steady blast of compressed thrust boosted the little barge from its berth and onto a trajectory to the sun. "Next stop incineration, gives a whole new meaning to the term vapors."

Millie switched to drone 134. "This is drone 134 equipped the same as 27 only with a deep space click sensor and 360 degree cameras mounted in four positions, top and bottom, front and rear. This bad boy here can record four different locations at once. Matter of fact drone 134 has seen war in many theatres of combat and managed to come out unscathed. Watch as I pan the cameras 360 degrees. Notice all the vessels moored here?" The cameras showed a vast docking system of several commercial ships including two deep space mining ships. But no Quincy 4 and Barge Omega.

"We'll route 134 through the moorings if drone 57 does not have Quincy 4 in sight." She switched to drone 57.

"Now what you're looking at are the active docks in what they refer to as the back of the Gate. Drone 57 is equipped with hard drive detection which will ping a hard drive for identification. So let's say we have a ship that has been destroyed or left unrecognizable for whatever reason. Drone 57 will simply align itself within fifty feet and scan or ping the hard drive and then it will be able to discern the ships identity. Here, let me show you on that derelict ship over there." She pointed to a large salvage ship, then maneuvered the drone in her direction.

"This is The Sandra K. salvage ship class "A" waiting to be stripped and launched into the sun. Her last salvage mission was the frigate SS Robertson which was attacked and unfortunately leaked its nuclear gel. Cost the crew their lives and the insurance company a few billion dollars. I think she's due for robotic propulsion within the next year. Real shame is, had she not been contaminated with nuclear gel, she wouldn't need to be scuttled." She was typing in coordinates for drone 57 when Franz spoke up.

"Can't be The Sandra K. Millie, according to the Gate workers the Sandra K. is almost to Gate 5 on an accelerated program."

"Hmmm, interesting," Millie said, not really paying much attention because she was busy now guiding drone 57.

"There we go, almost in position," she said.

Franz and Buck just looked at each other and shrugged.

Millie plugged a small device into her control computer, punched in a seven digit code and waited for the answer. Within thirty seconds she received an answer but it wasn't what she was expecting.

"Ummm, guys?" She said without looking up from her read out.

"Guys? If what I'm seeing is correct we have a real story on our hands."

Franz and Buck stopped watching the screen and turned towards Millie.

"What you got?" Franz asked.

"Well according to this hard drive detection we're looking at Quincy 4 but how can that be possible?"

"Can't be right, has to be a false reading or a prank or maybe Quincy 4 is hidden in a shadow somewhere behind The Sandra K. Send that drone over The Sandra K. and let's have a look see what's on the other side." Buck suggested.

"Going to take a minute, but here goes."

Both men watched the screen as the drone reversed itself, then started to float up casting a bright light on the hull of The Sandra K. She was a gray blue with streaks and splotches of black and silver. The silver color was a direct result of radiation leakage from The Robertson. The drone breached the top of The Sandra K. still illuminating her all the way to her port side. On the descending run the drone turned lights on in front and behind. The Sandra K was still being lit up but there was no ship big enough to be the Quincy 4 or Barge Omega on her port side, not even close.

"All the way around The Sandra K. my instruments kept telling me she was Quincy 4. If this is correct that means Quincy 4 has been hackjacked and the ship everyone thinks is The Sandra K now on an accelerated course to the sun is really Quincy 4." Millie Fisher stated with a light look of horror on her face.

Buck stood up and took command of the room.

"Before any information leaves this room, we have to be one hundred percent absolute this is what we're looking at. Millie....."

She had cut him off. "Already on it, going to take a few days to ping every ship here so I'm only going to do class A and any ship close to the size of Quincy. I figure another eight hours on the short side, twelve hours max. You two head out of here and take this recording with you. Do not and I repeat, do not place this recording or information on any computer linked with our network. The right person could break into our systems at work and blast this story all over the world in record time. If you have to purchase a secure computer do it. We'll get Paul to reimburse you later. I'll call as soon as we can confirm and we'll meet in the studio to see where we go from here. Remember guys ... 'mums' the word."

Buck grabbed his shoes, kissed Millie on the cheek, "you don't need to tell us to be quiet on this story, we want to retire just as badly as you do. See you in about twelve hours."

Franz followed him out the door.

Millie spent the next ten hours guiding drone 57 over and under just about every ship moored at Gate 3 until she finally realized a story probably out of her league as a reporter was about to break.

Kester Trewer became even more disoriented with the flood lights on. He laid there trying to muster up the strength to move again even though he didn't know which direction he was moving or which direction he should be moving. Hope was fading fast, he barely had the strength to lift his head when he managed to lift his hand to block the bright light. His breathing became extremely laborious and his excrement thick and black as tar. He knew these symptoms from the time when his Aunt Merriam died that his hour was close at hand. His mind drifted to a time when his mother was alive and home. When life was happy. He was about eleven years old, The Great Park as it was known, sat perched on the edge of the Pacific Ocean. Roller coasters that defied gravity, giant Ferris Wheels that touched the clouds. The sounds of laughter, people having fun. His mother and father walking hand in hand giving him enough lead to feel a little more grown up than he really was. The smell of cotton candy, yes! He could smell it now. The scent of cotton candy wafted past his nostrils and he wanted some. He reached his hand out farther, stretching it out trying to grab for the cotton candy but to no avail. Then his mind drifted to Christmas of that same year. The bright lights on the family Christmas tree. The colorful packages neatly stacked under it. His mother baking cookies in the kitchen. Again he could smell those cookies and reached his hand out to try to grab them. "Please, Mom, may I have a cookie now?" He mumbled. The sweet smell of sugar and flour baking in the oven mixed with the sugar frosting filled his nose.

Miller pushed the red button on the intercom system. "Hey lady, your guy is moving again. I don't know if you're going to make it while he's still alive though. He's looking pretty weak if you ask me."

Lisa grumbled under her breath. "No one asked you." Then turned her screen on inside her private quarters. She could tell he had very little time left alive. By this time Shooster and Manetti re-emerged from their berths to take a look. The two men stood on the bridge behind Miller.

"You ready for this?" Shooster asked Manetti

"No I'm not ready for this nor will I ever be. This is gonna take at least a solid day to cut through especially with a wind shield."

Jim Houtt came up with the only feasible plan to cut their way in to the barge. When he ran the plan through his personal computer he learned the odds of it being successful was at thirty five percent. He's faced worse odds than that and came out smelling like a rose.

The plan consisted of a steel lid one inch smaller in circumference than the duct work. After the fourth screen is cut out the steel plate goes up with welded brackets on the ship side to prevent the disc from shooting out backwards. Once the fan is removed, the steel disc will be drilled according to the pressure needing to be regulated then welded in place. Shooster, Manetti and Lark literally sealing themselves outside the ship with four more screens to cut through. The whole time they're pushing the fan in front of them so they'll have it with them to re-install it on the way back out. Ingenious plan if there ever was one he thought. His next thought was we're all dead anyhow, we might as well die when this ship implodes. Houtt and Miller were summoned to the main deck mechanical room and to bring the keys to the lifts with them.

The four men stood there glaring at Lisa Lark with deadly contempt in their eyes.

"I know guys," she said. "Trust me, I don't want to do this anymore than you. However, just so we know. If something should happen to me in there it won't change a thing and my personal computer is collecting audio, visual and biological data throughout this entire ordeal. If you harm me or kill me you better hope Lewis isn't bluffing and this ship really is a ghost ship."

"Personally ma'am," Manetti spoke up. "I would not trust you further than the vacuum in space could suck you out. Let's do this thing if we're gonna do it. You wait here until we get the first screen cut out then we'll send the lift back down for you."

Manetti gave her a wink which she took as an assault on her femininity. "Take us up Jim."

Houtt turned the key to green and the platform that held Manetti, Shooster and the set of torches made its thirty-five foot journey to the grate which hid the first of eight screens to be cut out. The lift stopped, Shooster held the torch head up for Manetti to light and with a bright phosphorescent ball of fire he began to cut through the first screen. The inch think steel cut pretty easily; however, there were twenty- eight cuts required to completely remove the screen. When it was finally severed through entirely, it weighed close to a hundred and twenty pounds. Still glowing red hot where the last few cuts were made, Manetti elbowed Shooster with an evil grin on his face. He pushed the screen to the edge of the platform then tipped it off with the heel of his protective boot.

"Heads up," he yelled as the screen crashed to the floor in an explosion of sparks and noise. "You ok Miss Lady Boss?" He yelled down at Lisa. "Whatever you do don't touch that, it's still red hot and you really should be more careful where you stand when men are working above you."

She mumbled under her breath "you got that right." She gave Manetti an angry glare with a thumbs up to signify she was ok.

"Bring us down Jim." Shooster hollered.

The platform quietly made it's slow decent to ground level. Manetti slid the safety chain from its hooks, "break time, I need a cup of coffee." He and Shooster stepped off the platform and headed towards the mess hall.

"Hold on just a second." Ms. Lark demanded. "We got a full day's work ahead of us and you're taking a coffee break after one hour?"

"Look lady," this time it was Miller who spoke up. "That torch is a phosphorescent cutting torch. It can handle any job you can imagine; however it cuts at twelve thousand degrees and leaves behind a dripping slag. Until that hole is cool enough to safely go through, it's time for coffee. You can challenge us on this all you want but I know those two won't be going back up for at least half an hour."

She stormed to the mess hall, "I'll give you guys twenty minutes and then we go back up, got it?"

Houtt chuckled and turned to Manetti, "she's kind of pretty when she's mad, huh?"

Manetti's reply was, "I still think she's nuts."

Chapter 10

(Kester's body)

"So, how do you want to spin this story?" Paul Downing asked his three reporters. "What are the facts you have and what facts can you broadcast without compromising the network." He was looking at Millie so she figured she should be answering his questions.

"Fact: we know Kester Trewer is missing."

"Fact: we know there was human tissue and blood left at Governor Trewer's mansion that was not Kester Trewer's."

She was interrupted by her boss. "Can you confirm this?" he asked.

"We have a source.... we think," she answered. Then continued.

"Fact: we know Quincy 4 is nowhere near Gate 3."

"How do you know this?" her boss quipped. "I mean it could be near Gate 3, good chance it's not, but still it could be."

Millie shot him the hairy eyeball, "Ok ... Fact: we sent three drones to Gate 3 to look for Quincy 4 and all three drones came up empty."

Paul Downing stood up to address his reporters. "It's like this, we're sitting on a huge story that sooner or later someone else will figure out. Just so happens that someone is us. When this story goes out, I want us to be sitting pretty with it. All those other networks sent drones and reporters to Gate 4 and every person in this room knows beyond a shadow of a doubt that tug is not going to stop there. Please continue Millie"

Millie glanced up from her notes and gave her boss a crooked smile.

"Fact: we pinged every hard drive on every class A ship at Gate 3 and found the derelict deep space mining vessel The Sandra K. to be posing as Quincy 4."

"Fact: according to log books and manifest entries The Sandra K. is due for her last voyage in three days, which means if we don't break the story within seventy two hours we'll lose it because all our facts will be headed to the sun."

"You know how we're going to spin this story Paul, and when we do it will be a great piece. We'll go back to our source but the man is fearful for his life. Now you need to tell me, what kind of protection can we offer him? You know as well as I know if we offer him nothing we get nothing. Off the record and strictly off the record our source feels Governor Trewer knows something about the disappearance of his son. I mean let's face it. Kester Trewer has been a national embarrassment to us and a personal embarrassment to the Governor. It's no secret Governor Trewer has his sights set on higher office and what better way to achieve higher office than by eliminating your greatest obstacle and gathering the sympathy of the voters in one fail swoop?"

Paul Downing, Director in Chief of the Global Broadcast Company stood up to address his reporters. He first pointed at Franz Hummel, "you have anything to add?"

Franz shook his head, "I'll see if I can get my source to go on record, other than that suicide mission, I got nothing else."

Paul pointed at Buck Whistler, "what about you Buck, you got anything else?"

"Not at the moment," Buck answered

"Well, lady and gentlemen we go public in twelve hours. Get your facts in order and I'll see if I can find a judge to put a temporary cease and desist restraining order on The Sandra K." He gathered his notes and started to walk out the door, when he stopped, turned back to face his crew. "One more thing ... find out who owns The Sandra K." He disappeared into the waves of the hustle and bustle of the news room.

"I got that one," Buck said and now if you'll excuse me, we have work to do. The three reporters went their separate ways.

Lisa Lark was sitting about twenty feet inside the duct work. She was totally exhausted and nursing a phosphorous burn on her right hand. Again the extraction crew as they now have come to be called, was in a resting situation waiting for the third screen to cool off enough to move it out of the way. It was Ms. Lark's job to push the screens in sections of two each with her feet until she toppled them out of the duct work. She made the painful mistake in her eagerness, she inadvertently latched on to the third screen while it was still hot. The smell of her heavy gloves, the phosphorescent slag and her burning flesh encompassed the shaft they were working in and both men knew immediately what had happened. Manetti squeezed his way past Shooster to find Lisa rocking back and forth in the duct work about fifteen feet from the opening.

"Let me take a look," he said to her as he reached out for her hand.

"I guess I never realized just how bad a phosphorescent burn can be." She said as she held her hand out then quickly retracted it. "Don't try to remove my glove, I think it's burned into my flesh. I'll look at it at the end of the day, for now I just wish I had something for the pain."

Manetti gently rolled the gloved hand over to look at the wound. "The good news about a burn from this much heat is, the wound cauterized itself. Very little chance of infection. I'll message Houtt and ask him to lift up some pain meds and next time you're out there, grab em. You need to tell me though if you're experiencing any disorientation or dizziness. I'm not gonna lie to you, this is a very serious injury and quite frankly short of sedation, the pain meds we have on board won't be much help." Manetti knew she would die trying before she would allow that injury to stop them.

He made his way back to Shooster who was about ready to cut the last screen on the ship's side.

"How is it?" he asked Manetti.

"Pretty bad, she won't be able to use that hand at all. She was lucky she didn't lose it all together.   What really stinks is ... now we got a gimp going in there with us."

Shooster pulled his eye protection down, Manetti followed suit and the cutting torch popped back to life and started showering the area with more sparks and dripping slag.

Millie Fisher was catching a little cat nap when her phone started to beep. She programmed the device to alert her through drone 57 in case anything out of the ordinary was taking place. The digital voice message said. "*Alert deep space mining vessel The Sandra K now carrying Interstellar Tug Quincy 4's identification information has just commenced compressing its thrust tanks. The Sandra K will be fully compressed in eighteen hours sixteen minutes and twenty three seconds and counting. The vessel will be moving in to launch position in less than twenty four hours.*" The message repeated itself twice, however Millie Fisher didn't sit still long enough to hear it again. She was too busy gathering her notes and sources and dashing out the door while trying to reach her boss. She was convinced now that Kester Trewer or at least his body was on board The Sandra K. and that the ship acted out of defense and started an automatic thrust compression and launch sequence after drone 57 pinged her computer identification. She feared twenty four hours from now all hope of finding that out would be lost.

Paul Downing was woken up from his nap too, this time by Millie's frantic phone call.

"How you coming along with that judge boss? Cause I gotta tell you there's something going on here and it stinks. I was just alerted that The Sandra K is currently compressing thrust and due to launch in twenty four hours. We, or should I say I, must have triggered an automatic engage of some kind when I pinged her. I'll buy the entire staff dinner if I'm wrong on this one, but I'll bet you Kester Trewer's body is on that ship. I mean what else could it be?"

He could detect the urgency in her voice as he checked to see if he had a message from the judge.

"I still don't have it. No word back yet." he said.

"Well you best be giving him or someone else another call. I'll be in the conference room in about twenty minutes. I've already called Franz and Buck, they're in route as we speak. Make sure you have the best anchor we got ready. As soon as the restraining order comes through, we'll be going to a live feed."

Beads of sweat steamed down Lisa Larks face, her hair was wet and stringy. She was about to go in to shock from the pain in her hand and was not about to tell Manetti and Shooster. The extraction team finally reached the fan which was still stabilizing the air pressure into and out of the barge. The stench was starting to become intense. Each screen was backed by a filter system made of a light weight cotton like material. Now half of that material lay in a heap mixed with cut up metal on the floor of the mechanical room.

"She's hurt pretty bad." Shooster said to Manetti.

"Don't remind me man, as it is I think we're going to be on our own here real soon." Manetti answered back.

Manetti messaged Houtt to cut the power to the fan. Shooster struggled to drag in the thick metal disk to seal up the hole where the fan now sits. He drilled several holes in the plate steel to assure some type of positive air flow.

"You ready?" Shooster asked Manetti.

Manetti stalled for a minute then said. "You know what? If something goes wrong in here and we need to move out fast we're either gonna have to move what's her name out of the way or drag her sorry butt with us." He nodded in the direction of Detective Lark who was now shivering in a cold sweat from the pain.

"Any suggestions?" Shooster asked.

"I'm thinking we take a break, crawl back to the lift and take her to sick bay. Grab some grub, hydrate and head back, in about an hour or two. Personally, I would love to get out of these sweat soaked clothes and grab some fresh gloves, too."

"Works for me." Shooster said. He then messaged Houtt again to hold off on cutting the power. Both men turned to exit the duct work. They were at least forty feet back in when they were met by a hand gun pointed at them. Lisa Lark went from shivering to shaking violently from the pain of her injury. Shooster froze, Manetti chuckled then said "a stray bullet in here hits that fan no one gets out alive." He crawled on his hands and knees to where Lisa was resting against the duct work. He reached out, gently removed the gun from her hand. "Shoe and I are going to take you to sick bay, non-negotiable. You'll be dead before we breach the other side and believe it or not, no one here wants that. So just relax and we'll do our best to get you out quickly."

Manetti positioned himself behind Lisa's back and Shooster grabbed her legs.

"On three" he said. When they lifted her up, she let out a deafening scream and then went into shock. The two men moved as quickly as they could, waddling back through the duct work. When they reached the cavernous mechanical room, Houtt and Miller were both waiting on the platform of the lift to lend a hand.

By the time they got her to sick bay she was unconscious. They removed her protective clothing and laid her out on a bed. Every mission required at least one member to have a medical certificate. Miller was the lucky one. He started to scan her vital signs but something was wrong. It was making no sense. She had a fever of 105.8 from a phosphorescent burn? Maybe a slight fever, nothing over 100.5 but this was serious. He punched his medical code into the ships on board access, then typed in a few words and within seconds a clear plastic tub was filled with forty five gallons of ice cold water. He instructed Manetti and Houtt to remove all her clothes except the glove that was burned into her flesh. Stripped naked the four men carried her to the tank of cold water and slid her in. Her eyes shot open wide in horror and she started to splash about and scream, trying to get out.

"Hold on Lark, you need to calm down," Miller said. He ordered the other three men to hold her down. Lisa thrashed and splashed around in the ice cold water like a fish trying to break free from a hook. When she finally succumbed to the emersion her temperature dropped rapidly and she started to beg Miller to let her out of the water.

"Hang with me for just one more minute," he told her. He went to grab some towels and a robe. "I know you're gonna wanna stand up on your own but the four of us are gonna help you out. Wrap these towels around you if you like."

"Kind of late for that now isn't it?" she sarcastically bit back her lips, now a nice shade of cold blue. "You guys get a good look?"

"Matter of fact we did," quipped Shooster. "We got a good look at a woman who was two steps from dead and now all she can do is worry about if we seen her happy hoo ha or not." Shooster had finally had enough and once he reaches that point he becomes the proverbial bull in a china shop. He extended his index fingers while his eyebrows raised. "You compromised that whole deal lady, we spent six hours in that duct work because you told us we had to. Then you point a gun at us when we tried to save your life. Let me tell you something, miss two steps from dead, you aint been on board this ship long enough to treat us like that. Yeah were gonna go in there and tromp through the garbage for someone who hasn't moved a muscle in the last twenty four hours. You better get this straight through your thick skull. You want us to perform like the circus then at least feed us peanuts...." Houtt and Miller burst out laughing then stepped in to stop him.

"Feed us peanuts?" Houtt asked him.

"Yeah well I'm upset with this mission, with this ship, and with that woman," pointing to Detective Lark. "It was all I could think of saying."

Even the Detective had a smile on her face. "Ok guys, I get it, and I'm sorry and thank you all for saving me. I have no idea what happened, one minute I'm good the next I'm burned and the last thing I remember is getting dunked in that freezing water. I don't think I can ever convince you men of the importance of bringing back Kester Trewer's body. By now you must have realized I'm also not buying what Frank Lewis is selling about us being doomed. That sort of thing doesn't happen in the twenty-fourth century and I don't care if we have been Hackjacked and I don't care if we did A.M.P. too soon and I don't even care that we loaded the cubes on that drone.... again I say, this sort of thing just does not happen in this day and age. Somehow we're getting off this ship." By now a little flush of color crossed her face. "You men take your break and I'll...."

She was cut off by Houtt. "You'll do jack squat Ms. Lark, I have top seniority on this ship and Manetti is a close second, we know what you need and no one else, including you, is going to jeopardize another living being on this ship again. We got this, now if you'll excuse us, we need to eat and Miller needs to find out what's wrong with you." Houtt then placed a hand on each of Shooster's and Manetti's shoulders and walked them out of the sick bay.

"She does have a pretty nice happy hoo ha though." Shooster said on the way out.
"Hey Mister, I heard that." Lisa yelled after them.

Miller instructed Lisa to sit on the examination table, rolled the x-ray machine over and took a few pictures. Lisa watched on the screen as the images started to appear.

"Is that a piece of phosphorus embedded in my hand?" She asked.

"Yep that's exactly what that is, and judging by the veins that have been cauterized, you're probably experiencing systemic phosphorescent blood poisoning. Never seen it happen that fast before but if that's the case we're looking at surgery to remove the contaminant and then about four hours on a blood filter and time is not on our side."

"Then I guess we should get this show on the road." She told him.

The Sandra K.

The Sandra K:, a class A deep space mining ship. Used by the Mining Consortium of UMA (United Miners Association). Canadian owned and operated out of C-Gate 3. Class A ships are known for speed and stealth. Mainly used as an escort to track or follow a hauler on a return trip. The mining of comets has become quite a lucrative business and piracy became equally lucrative. She became derelict when she salvaged the Robertson after it floundered leaving the ore mine of Mansfield fourteen and became contaminated with nuclear gel. Apparently, when the crew charged the thrust the return line was worn just enough to blast a hole in it. When the thrust escaped from the hole instead of the thrust injector it caused the ship to move sideways resulting in a collision with the comet.

Most likely purchased for a high speed interceptor or escort ship for the Canadian mining industry. The ship was scheduled for repairs on the mechanics docks at C-Gate 3 but the paper trail ends there. No record of the repair and no manifest. After six months a ship with no manifest becomes the property of the Gate where that ship is berthed as salvage rights. Funny how the Canadian emblem is still proudly displayed on both sides of the ship. Another funny thing about The Sandra K was she was refitted with six external boosters. Usually external boosters are either for catching another ship or out running one. Somehow Buck figured this ship was going to be outrunning something or someone. He dug a little deeper checking the manufacturer's numbers against the serial number. The Sandra K. was built by General Flight and Thrust. A company whose roots can be traced back to twenty second century Earth and the pioneering of gravity breaking acceleration. This particular ship has the code series of

12R12R in her serial number. This told Buck the ship was built by the Russians in 2312. The original bill of sale said she was first purchased by Indian Royalty. Prince Yuni Nagan. The prince logged only a handful of flights before the ship was sold to the manufacturing corporation Simcoa. Simcoa, back in the day manufactured synthetic oxygen components. It was an extremely profitable business up until the explosion. Simcoa used the ship as a warehouse for potential customers. Buck skipped through all the purchases from Simcoa to present. He went straight for the last buyer. The last purchase of The Sandra K. was to the Canadians. Buck followed the money trail of this purchase and low and behold, there it was in black and white. Barry Wells's name was on the bill of sale along with six other board members. A quick search on Barry Wells turned up a photo of the Canadian Prime Minister shaking hands with none other than Governor Roman Trewer.

"Bingo." Buck muttered under his breath. "Now we have to figure out why?"

The three reporters all met back at the station with their perspective findings. Millie and Franz were both impressed with Buck's findings and agreed they needed to find out what this was all about.

"Hey Chief, how we doing on that restraining order?" Millie asked.

"I think we're close," Paul said. "I just hope we can get it in time. What'd you guys find out?"

Millie suggested they meet in person in one of the safe rooms at the station and go over all the details.

Within fifteen minutes Paul Downing was on his way to personally see the judge with new information.

Miller had just finished cleaning Lisa's wound when Houtt, Manetti and Shooster reappeared and prepared to go back to tunneling their way into the barge.

"She gonna live?" Shooster asked.

"Yes Mr. Shooster, looks like I'm going to make a full recovery." She answered for Miller.

Holding up her hand Shooster noticed it was wrapped in white gauze with no blood stain.

"Skinthetic?" He asked Miller.

"Yea, it was her decision, I didn't even know she knew the stuff existed. She asked me to hold off on the surgery and she'll have it done when she gets off the ship. Unfortunately, she was at great risk for phosphorescent blood poisoning so I had to go in and remove the piece of slag. It was embedded pretty deep but I got it all."

Lisa tried to sit up and Miller placed his arm across her breasts and slightly motioned for her to lay back down.

"You aint going nowhere. We'll keep you posted and according to the latest update, we have another four to five hours of cutting before we reach the barge and who knows how long until we reach your man."

Lisa sighed, huffed and puffed a little but relented. then laid back down.

Manetti shook his head and mumbled. "That crazy broad still thinks we're getting off this ship."

Houtt walked away, he wanted to check the infrared one more time before they had to shut down those systems. He also wanted to scan the barge one more time with the cameras just for a reference point. He had been sitting on the bridge for about twenty minutes when Shooster and Manetti finally caught up to him.

"Tell me you're gonna pull rank and put a stop to this madness." Manetti put Shooster up to saying.

"Not a flippin thing I can do about it. You guys know that. Please let's not get started on something we can't finish. Our best bet is to climb our happy butts back in the tunnel and start cutting. I'll get you two started then come back here so I can switch the fans off and on at the right times. But Hey! Look at the bright side, if we can't equalize that pressure within ten PSI the whole thing will implode and you'll be right Manetti." Houtt never bothered to look up at the two men when he said that.

Shooster and Manetti walked off the lift and started to duck walk back into the tunnel where the first dual fan was.

"The moment of no return, Shoe my boy." Manetti said as he looked at the spinning fan.

"We have about an hour to remove this fan and place this steel plate here. How many holes do you think we need to drill?"

Shooster removed his digital reader from his pocket and started to punch in some numbers.

"According to my calculations if we just cut one hole thirty three and a half inches in circumference that should be about as perfect as we can get."

"Only one hole and not several small holes?" Manetti asked in protest.

"That's what I have here, take a look." Shooster showed the formula to Manetti.

"You do realize Shoe, once we cut this fan out and place this metal here we'll be on the other side with nowhere to go, but in?"

"Yeah! I got that part, no need to remind me again." Shooster barked back. "I'm just as stressed out over this as you are and this is one time I don't need the pot stirred. You just do your job and I'll do mine, got it?"

"Sorry man, I don't like it any more than you do. I'm about to puke as it is," Manetti said.

"Yea well don't puke here, we have to work in this area for another hour, and then another hour on the way back." POP! He lit the torch.

Houtt's radio crackled "Ok Jim, kill the fan."

Both men in the tunnel felt the change in the wind and temperature immediately. But what they did not expect was the deep moaning of the heavy ship when the air pressure changed.

"I think you better hurry up Shoe." Manetti chuckled with a slight quiver of fear in his voice.

Shooster hit the first bracket with the torch and started to cut.

"One down and five to go," he said.

Manetti checked his watch, it took only three minutes to cut the bracket. That was the good news. The bad news came when the fan was completely cut out and they had to move it. Much to their horror they discovered there was only room for one piece to be moved. They could move the fan or they could move the plate but they couldn't move both without backing the plate all the way out, remove it then do the same for the fan. Manetti removed his gloves and ran his hands from his brow over his bald head to wipe the sweat and contemplate going completely insane. All of a sudden Shooster popped the torch back on and started to cut the thick steel plate right down the middle. Before Manetti could even stop him he was a good six inches in.

Shooster yelled over the din of the torches, "It's the only way I can see us moving forward."

Manetti pointed to the second steel plate for the second fan and suggested Shooster cut that one too. This only enhanced their fear, seeing no choice in the matter this was the easy part. Not knowing how to cut it to adjust the air flow was another story. Nonetheless he cut both plates. He pushed the four halves through the fan opening and climbed in behind them.

"Coming?" he asked Manetti, adding, "don't burn yourself on those hot spots."

Manetti climbed through, grabbed one half of the steel plate, held it in place and Shooster tack welded it. He repeated the process with the second half and as soon as it was tacked in place the ship let out another creaking moan as the air pressure made its way almost back to normal. Another fifteen feet found the two men at the second fan and Shooster once again calculating the sizes and numbers of holes required to keep the ship from imploding. The smell of the garbage was now so overwhelming Manetti started to gag.

Back on the bridge, Houtt could find no signs of life larger than the occasional rat scurrying over some undetectable pile of garbage. He scanned left to right then front to back and still nothing. It could be quite possible that the life form whatever it is, either died or was buried so deep in garbage it was undetectable.

By the time Manetti and Shooster reached the second fan they were officially outside the body of Quincy 4. This meant there was only a six - inch layer of steel wrapped in another three inches of insulated composite that separated them from the cold vacuum of space. The two men welded the next two sections of steel plate in place. This plate required four holes, nine inches in diameter, and Manetti could swear he saw the shaft wall buckle slightly when the ship let out another protesting grumble and moan. Ahead of them lay three more steel grates then they would be inside the garbage barge.

Lisa forced herself out of sick bay and joined Miller and Houtt on the bridge. "How's it looking guys?" She asked.

"Your man must be dead by now." Houtt replied. "There's no sign of life. Watch when I pan this camera."

Houtt panned the camera and zoomed in on an image. "Does that look like a foot sticking out the end of something to you? Not to mention the infra-red showed nothing before I had to shut it down."

Lisa peered in closer to the screen. "Yep that's what that looks like to me. So how do you explain the live or should I say alive image we saw days before?"

"I can't, I have no way of explaining that either. Maybe we just wanted to see someone alive. Maybe it was a mass hallucination. Stranger things have happened in space you know. All I know is, if that's your body there, it's been dead for a long time."

"How much further until our guys reach the barge?" She asked.

"Last I heard they still had two more grates to cut through, that was about forty minutes ago."

Just as Houtt finished that sentence his radio crackled.

"Hey Sparky, you got a copy?" Shooster said.

"Yea Shoe, I copy, what's up?"

"We're through and we're looking at about two cubic miles of putrid slimy garbage through dim lights. Man we can't see squat. I don't suppose that happy hoo ha lady even understands what she's asking us to do. There better be a bonus in this for us." Shoe's voice was condescending at best.

"Um, yeah, Shoe, the happy hoo ha lady is sitting right next to me here." Houtt said.

"Good! Good place for her. Better you than me buddy that's all I have to say."

Those on the bridge could here Manetti in the back ground saying. "A bonus won't do us no good when we get vaporized by the sun. Maybe we should, at the very least, have Ms. Happy Hoo Ha send instructions out in space for our families to get the bonus. Maybe it will get picked up by some honest sympathetic sap and be delivered back home."

Lisa cleared her throat while grabbing the microphone from Houtt's hand. "Ok boys, enough with the Happy Hoo Ha lady crap. I need to know what you need and what you see."

Shooster answered again. "We need some stinking light up in this grill lady. We got like literally two cubic miles to search and four flood lights on. Tell Sparky to hit the main breakers and pray they all work." There was a low hum followed by a small halo of light starting to flicker. Each light made a pop sound when it finally reached its brightest illumination. "Pop, pop, pop, pop"..... In rapid succession until all the working flood lights were lit.

"That's a little better." Shooster called back on his radio.

The two men were both wearing back packs with food and medical supplies in each. Manetti removed his and pulled out a nylon rope ladder. When he pulled out the ladder, a nylon body bag fell out too. He quickly scooped it up and stuffed it back in. The plan was dead or alive they would put Kester's body (if it was Kester) in the bag then lift him up into the shaft to drag him back out. He unfurled the rope ladder and let it dangle into the abyss below.

"You first," he chuckled a command to Shooster.

Shooster slowly slid over the edge of the shaft opening, grabbed the rope ladder and immediately swung completely around to his left. Holding on with everything he had with his back now against the wall, this actually helped him to descend. At the bottom of the ladder he felt around for a footing, something solid to stand on. At first glance it was disbelief. At second glance it was worse. He managed to find a hard surface to rest his foot on but as soon as he put his weight on it, it collapsed. He slid down a little bit but managed to regain balance on the ladder with his hands. He looked up at Manetti. "I'm trying to find a place to stand here, I'll holler up when I do."

Thirty minutes later both men were standing on a pile of old clothes and trash bags surveying their surroundings. It reminded them of a cross between a rat maze and a jungle. And this was just the top, they were standing two hundred feet up from the floor.

Manetti turned to Shoe, "you ever seen the bad lands in South Dakota?"

"Never been there why?"

"Because this is exactly what this reminds me of. I have no idea how a settler ever got a horse drawn wagon through those Bad Lands. Its one small mountain after another for as far as the eye can see. Mountain up, valley down over and over. Black Hills Spruce trees by the millions. Rocks, boulders every natural obstacle now known by man. It had to be next to impossible to navigate."

"Ok Vince, I think you finally snapped. What does the bad lands of South Dakota have to do with this?"

"This is the bad lands of garbage." Manetti solemnly said.

Shooster just stood there looking out over the vast mountainous span of junk and garbage in disbelief.

"What am I doing here?" He asked to no one in particular except Manetti was standing there.

"We are in need of a miracle, because if not, we grossly underestimated how much food and water to bring."

Shooster just looked at Manetti with a dumbfounded look on his face. Manetti simply reached over, placed his hand under Shooster's chin and closed his mouth for him.

"I have food for two days and water for three between the two of us, if we stretch it maybe five days. Besides there's gotta be a rat or two running around so there's always hope." Even though Manetti was pretty sure he and Shooster were going to implode with the rest of garbage in about another three weeks anyhow.

Manetti's radio buzzed to life. "Hey guys, this is Lisa."

They both thought *who the heck else can it be?*

"I'll be in command now, what you need to do is walk on a three degree angle to your right about a hundred and seventy five feet or so. We're looking at a foot sticking out of something and I'm guessing this is our man. I'm also guessing he's been dead since the beginning and I apologize for putting you guys through this. Can you give me a thumbs up if you can see him?"

There was no affirmative signal from either Manetti or Shooster. Lisa didn't know if this was because they really can't see him or if because they just didn't feel like answering her. Nonetheless the men started their trek through the Bad Lands of Garbage.

Kester managed to get himself wedged upside down in some sort of composite tube about three feet in diameter and six feet deep. His breathing became so shallow he was inhaling maybe five or six times a minute. He felt no more pain but he could still smell the sickening sweet odor of rancid meat. This he concluded, was his own rotting flesh. He was right. His tongue was now stuck to the roof of his mouth being as dehydrated as he was and his decaying teeth became a choking hazard. His testicles retreated into his groin and what was left in his kidneys and bladder was the occasional bloodied drop of urine. The muscles in his legs seized up causing his tendons to contract, drawing his knees well into his chest. The occasional maggot dining on his chest wound would fall off and land on his face or in his mouth. He was just too weak to struggle with it despite the fact it was driving him insane. His arms still worked a little but there was just nothing left in him to fight for and yet his heart kept beating and his lungs kept drawing in oxygen thus defying the very mystery of death itself.

His first few months he was quite proficient when it came to finding food and managed to scrounge up several nearly full plastic bottles of water. After his second time around going through withdraws and delusional hallucinations he wondered how much time passed since he was tossed in the dumpster and left for dead. Judging by the beard on his face and length of his finger nails before they fell off a rough quesstimate would put it around five months. He finally had one regret in his life, that being he just didn't swallow all his dope from the start and save himself from the horrors of the last several weeks. But life is funny, it's the one thing he clung onto and yes he never understood why.

Now as he lay there staring up at the ceiling to the dumpster, he faded off into another dream state. This time in his dream he saw two men balance on a plank of wood they just laid across the top of the cylinder he was in. Then the same two men walked above him it like two tight rope walkers of days gone by then disappeared into the analogs of his mind. He brushed a few maggots off his face with what little strength he had left, closed his eyes and again drifted far, far away.

Paul Downing dropped a legal size folder on Judge Harmon's desk.

"We have Kester Trewer missing. An abandoned ship which now bares the electronic signature of Quincy 4. That same abandoned ship is registered to Canada more specifically a Canadian who goes by the name of Barry Wells. Barry Wells and Roman Trewer have been in bed together over the launching of trash to the sun thing since they've both been in office. And on top of that we have a tug... scuse me not just *a* tug but we have Quincy 4 on her last voyage now gone missing. She has been Hackjacked with The Sandra K and who knows what else. We have The Sandra K sitting in impound at Gate 3 and she's carrying the electronic signature of Quincy 4. Do you realize how many press and just plain old every day on lookers are patiently waiting for Quincy 4 to leave Gate 3 and she's not even there?"

The judge held up a silencing hand and motioned for Paul to sit down. He opened the folder and started to leaf through it. Finally he looked up.

"Do you have anybody at Gate 3 who can take a look into this matter personally Mr. Downing?"

"No sir, all we have are drones on site. We do have a crew in route though. I have three reporters who investigated this and while they were doing so I sent a crew out to the Gate. To be honest though your honor, that ship will be gone by the time they arrive. I'm guessing at least twenty hours head start. If you can issue this restraining order, maybe just maybe the ship will still be sitting there when my crew arrives. I give you my word, you will have one full day to go over everything we find before we break the story. But that offer starts now not ten minutes from now. You sign the order now and we'll alert security and they'll have The Sandra K locked down solid."

The judge restacked the papers in the file and leafed through them again. This time a little slower. He paused every now and then to read a line or two or to study a picture. He then laid the folder down on his desk, closed it, leaned in on his elbows.

"Were you working at your station during the riots Mr. Downing?"

"Yes." Paul answered. "I was on the streets reporting through most of it. I didn't move into my position for a few years after that. Why do you ask?"

"I'm going to sign your request. But before I do, I want to share a little story with you."

Paul looked at the clock on the wall then started tapping his right foot impatiently.

"Oh stop it and relax," Judge Hammond told him.

"That ship aint going anywhere between now and the next ten minutes. You see I was working the eighth district as a prosecutor at the time of the riots. I personally took the protestors side. I believe ridding the Earth of our garbage by Solar Incineration is stupid and arrogant. I'm sure you're aware of the depletion of reusable energy sources such as metals and papers because we lose so much of it in those barges. The cost associated with just the launches here in the U.S. are obscene. But I was stuck you see. I was an officer of the courts and bound to a higher standard than your average citizen. So my personal point of view was meaningless much as it remains today. I have to take in consideration all the evidence and then spit out a decision. No matter what that decision is, there will always be a loser. So I walk into my office one morning, the riots were just about to peak. Protesters lined the streets the whole way in. Sitting on my desk was a file. In that file were the names of twenty three people... protestors if you will. In red ink written across an 8x10 black and white mug shot of each person was the word execute. A clandestine group of police officers, men and women alike were sent out into the streets. Their job was to find these twenty three protestors and bring them in.... Quietly. My job was to prosecute them under falsified information and recommend the death penalty. I knew the sitting judge back then but you won't get his name out of me so don't ask. I knew he would sentence them to death. But not on my recommendation. On the orders of ... you guessed it Governor Roman Trewer. I was made a patsy that day. Did I recommend the death sentence for the twenty three? Yes. Did I sentence them to death that day? No. Nonetheless my name is on twenty three recommendations for the death penalty for twenty three citizens who were probably no more than out spoken political activists. Heck I bet if they were alive today, they would be living out a peaceful existence somewhere near the ocean watching every launch and toasting them with a shot of whiskey."

He then pulled the keyboard to his computer close to him. Made a few strokes on the key pad, behind him, his printer came to life and started to print the restraining order. Judge Hammond signed the order, handed it to Paul Downing then said. "If our Governor is behind this, I want to be the first person to know, got it?"

"Got it your Honor and thank you." As Paul stood up to leave, he heard the judge call in the restraining order and all Paul could do now was hope The Sandra K. would be powered down and still sitting there twenty hours from now when his crew arrived.

The white hazmat suits Shooster and Manetti were wearing offered very little protection at this stage. Both men were covered in stench and garbage from head to toe. It was all they could do not to laugh at each other to keep from throwing up. They'd been at this job now for over nineteen hours and they could see no end in sight.

"Hey Houtt, you got a copy?" Manetti's voice sounded distant and faint as it came through the radio.
"Yeah, I copy you, what'd you guys find?" Houtt asked back.

"Do you have a location on that foot sticking up and if so how close are we?"

"Near as I can figure out, you're about another two maybe two hundred and fifty feet away. I see you both on the camera but now the infra-red is down because the floods are on. Best I can do is just keep guiding you through."

They each had a plank ten feet long and two feet wide. This they kept placing across the debris piles and piles of putrid garbage. They would place one plank down then move the other plank ahead of them, taking a good fifteen minutes to move twenty feet.

"At this pace, we'll be in here for a week." Shooster mumbled to no one in particular.

He placed his plank across an old sofa which lead to a fifty five gallon composite drum that once held cooking oil. Little did he know that the sofa was once home to Kester Trewer. They never even bothered to look for clues or evidence of anything or anyone alive, both figuring this was a dead end journey anyhow, no pun intended. Manetti slid past Shooster on the plank, then reached back to grab the other. When he did, the plank they were standing on tipped sideways. This caused Manetti to lose grasp of the other plank and right before their eyes, it disappeared into the abyss of the garbage. Shooster ended up on the sofa and Manetti, not being so lucky ended up in what once was a pile of peaches and several meals for Kester. He managed to find a place to plant his feet and then stood up. Shooster tried to control himself but the laughter poured out.

"I've had it, I'm done with this crap. You go find our needle in the hay stack, but I'm not taking another step." He screamed at Shooster.

"Fine by me" Shoe answered back. "But just where do you think you're going? We're stuck in here and you know it. Most likely we'll die in here too. Ole miss happy hoo ha is gonna see to that for us. There is no one alive in here and I'm tellin you right now, I refuse to drag a dead body back to the ship. Matter of fact, I have never even seen a dead body outside of a casket. Now if you're done yelling at me, let me remind you, I'm in this terlet bowl with you. Now we need that plank, you dropped it, you go after it." Shooster told Manetti with a dead grin and raised eye brows. Manetti was more mad about the fact he knew it needed to be found and they needed to carry on than he was about being covered in moldy fermented peach slim. He positioned himself above the hole the plank slid through, turned on his head lamp and descended. He squeezed his way past the back of the sofa dangling until he could stretch his legs long enough to find something to place his feet on, then let go and dropped. When he caught his balance unbeknownst to him he was standing on Kester's old clothes. Through the din, his light shown down a narrow passage of card board boxes and the frame work of discarded organic crates. Disposal of those crates on the outside cost a fortune, Manetti figured a friend or relative of a dock worker made a little extra scratch when they got dumped here. He wiggled his way down passed the frames and could barely get a finger hold on the plank. He needed at least another foot to reach it. He placed his left foot on the side angle of one of the frames, bent down and stretched his arm as far as he could. He felt the steady drip of something rotten and decomposing on his hazmat hood and was not interested in the slightest to find out what it was. Finally he wrapped his hand around the end of the plank and picked it up. By the time he lifted it up to Shooster he was about fourteen feet below the sofa. Shooster grabbed the plank, secured it in front of him then dropped Manetti a cable. Both men struggled to raise him back up and once they did, they sat on the sofa to catch their breath.

Hours later Shooster was looking at his first dead body outside of a casket when they reached what was left of Porter. Much to his astonishment Porter's body was not as hideous as he thought a dead body should be.
"This one's been dead awhile," Manetti said.

Shooster picked a small plastic pole and started poking the corps. "Who do you think this is?" He asked. He moved the dead man's shirt aside to expose a rib laden chest where most of the flesh had long since decayed. "You think this is our man?"

"Not sure," Manetti answered. "Everyone including Frank saw a live body in here and this poor sap has not been alive since we left Earth... if not longer. Let me see that stick." Manetti held out his hand towards Shooster. He took the stick and rolled the boney carcass over on its side. He tapped the back pocket of the dead man's trouser with the stick.

"Looks like our man might have an ID on him." Reaching down he slid a wallet from the back pocket and as he did he noticed the back side of the dead man had been eaten clean by something and the bones were left to be scavenged by maggots.

Just then both men's radios crackled to life. This time it was Lisa. She was watching the whole scene unfold through the cameras attached to their head lamps. "That's not our guy." She said.

Manetti read the identification card from Porters wallet then handed it to Shooster. Shooster looked up towards the back wall where they entered the barge holding the ID card at arm's length. "Name's Myra Porter," he said. "And his ID card has prison issue stamps on it. Looks like this guy crossed the wrong person."

He handed the card back to Manetti who placed it back in the wallet. Then he faced the same back wall, held his arms up in a what's up with that motion and asked, "Ok lady what next?" His radio crackled back. "Keep looking I know our man is in there somewhere."

Now it was Shoe's turn to have enough, he was close to snapping and started yelling in his radio.

"Are you totally insane lady? Here we are months into a death trip. We got one dead body in here already. (Truth is dead bodies were quite common place in dumpster barges.) We're standing in garbage, we had to cut our way in here and we'll have to cut our way back out. No one but you even believes we'll ever see our loved ones again and you say keep looking? Keep looking! Yeah well look at this lady. He placed his hands around his mouth and started yelling. "Oh Kester where are you? Here Kester Kester Kester. Come out and play Kester. Can you hear me Kester?" He started stomping around in a small circle of discarded cans and paper going ape. "Can you hear me, I'm calling you Kester, come on out now. All you all outs in free." Any semblance of sanity seemed to vaporize for Shooster. He started kicking trash around, some went scattering to the right, some to the left, some papers and wood splinters shot up in the air then fluttered down like a perverted snowfall. There was now a fine mist of decayed particles floating in the air and the stench was becoming unbearable but Shooster wasn't finished yet. He reached down and started to grab the garbage by the hand full and scattering it every which way. Like a dog burying a bone, he was sifting the garbage behind him between his legs. Manetti stood there with his t-shirt pulled up around his nose and mouth in stunned disbelief. *Shooster finally cracked, and I'm stranded in here with him,* he thought. Then as quickly as he started he stopped. With the tips of his fingers bleeding he picked up a plank, placed across another pile, turned to look at a very amused and slightly scared Manetti. "You coming?"

Without saying a word Manetti grabbed his plank, balanced himself behind Shooster and handed it off to him. It was a delicate ballet of balance the two men performed. Shooster would lay down his plank first, walk across it. Then Manetti would follow behind then hand Shooster his plank. Shooster would then place Manetti's plank down and move forward. Manetti lastly picked up the plank they just crossed and hand it back to Shooster. Hand over fist they made their way to another location in the garbage. They decided on a zigzag pattern from back to front working their way to the duct they crawled out of. At least then if they couldn't find him they better positioned themselves to exit the barge.

"I think our best bet is to back track about fifty feet, then make our way to the left side. From there we can walk the welded edge on the parameter to the back. What do you think?" Manetti asked Shooster.

"I think we'll be in here forty days and forty nights trying to find someone who is probably sitting on a beach somewhere in South America stoned out of his mind. I also think we out number Miss Hooha and we should just toss her happy butt in lock down with Frank when and if we ever get out of here."

The ear bud in Manetti's right ear crackled to life. "Not even funny as a joke, sir." Lisa's voice echoed in his ear. "You tell Shooster for me, that kind of language is taken as a threat and I won't tolerate it again." Manetti pushed the little button on the breast switch of his head set and said, "Hold on a second." He removed the head set, tapped Shoe on his shoulder. Shooster held up a balled fist in a military fashion and without looking back at Manetti and said. "Hold on, let me place this plank down." Shooster carefully placed the plank over the top of cylindrical object before cautiously and slowly turning to see what Manetti wanted. Manetti was standing just a few feet behind him holding out the headset.

"I think she wants to ask you out on a date," he said with a smile, as he handed the headset over. He could tell by the look on Shooster face, there was about to be another ballistic explosion of Neanderthal expression.

"What!?" Shooster asked in the microphone.

"Mr. Shooster, let me remind you who you are working for. I will no longer be the target for your or anyone else's misguided temperament. From this moment forward any lashing out at me verbally or physically will be met with a serious discipline. Do you understand me sir?"

At the phrase misguided temperament she lost Shooster to the Neanderthal within.

He bellowed back in his mic a string of words about labor unions, seniority and job descriptions that only made sense to him.

While Shooster was busy posturing his lack of anything intelligent to say, Manetti reached down in the garbage and pulled up a piece of paper. The context of the paper was irrelevant. All that mattered was the size. "Perfect," he mumbled to himself. He folded the piece of paper into an airplane. The model his Father taught him when he was a young boy. They called it *The Boom Air Rang*. The paper was folded into a winged flyer designed to always return to its thrower. Manetti passed the time trying to ignore Shooster's ongoing losing debate by flying his little toy. He launched it, it flew out over the garbage and returned close enough for him to reach out and catch. Just as Shooster explicitly told Lisa where the sun don't shine, he impatiently reached out and grabbed for the returning paper aircraft in an attempt to intercept it. This caused the plank to wobble and while both men were throwing their arms out to their sides to regain their balance, the *Boom Air Rang* flew down into the cylindrical object and gently struck an almost dead Kester Trewer in the forehead.

Both men being busy screaming and arguing or ignoring the one who was screaming and arguing, neither of them heard the faint banging on the cylinder. The whole time Shooster was being his true Neanderthal self, Kester Trewer was using his good arm and every last ounce of strength to try to alert the men of his presence.

"Shhhh, you hear something?" Manetti asked.

"I don't hear a thing other than my heart thumping in my chest, but I gave it to her good, didn't I? She didn't know what to say, I never gave her a word edge wise...." Shooster was cut off by Manetti slapping him in the chest with the back of his hand.

"Listen." He said with a still about him. "There it is again."

A faint metallic ting could be heard now.

"Where is it coming from?" Shooster asked while scanning the vast expanse of garbage.

"Almost sounds as if....."

Manetti started to look down at his feet.

"It's coming from..."

He flipped his small forehead lamp on.

"Down here."

He pointed to his feet that were perched atop the plank of wood. And when he bent down to look, Kester Trewer was immediately blinded by the high intensity of the head lamp. He could only close his good eye at that point considering the other was matted shut from the mucus and blood seeping out of it.

Twelve hours later both men found themselves showered and scarfing down everything in sight in the mess hall.

Chapter 11

Media Coverage

You're on in, 3, 2, 1 the man with a head set on pointed his finger at Lowell Harding the leading GBC news anchor.

"Good evening ladies and gentlemen, I'm Lowell Harding and this is the news." He was perched behind a futuristic counter with the station insignia embossed in 3D over a depiction of a softly back lit planet Earth washed in blue light trimmed in chrome. His tie was straight and not a hair out of place as he looked directly into the camera.

"Ladies and Gentlemen, as you know there has been an ongoing concern over the whereabouts of Kester Trewer, the only and sometimes troubled son of Governor to the Planet, Roman Trewer. We here at Global Broadcast Company have this exclusive breaking story. This is a story with several twists and turns, but trust me when I say ladies and gentlemen, you simply just cannot make this stuff up. Follow closely. The Governor's son came up missing about the same time the famed Quincy 4 embarked on its final mission. As you also know, Quincy 4 is scheduled to be scuttled into the sun. What we have just learned is, this famed ship has been Hackjacked with a class A mining ship named The Sandra K. The Sandra K. is also scheduled to be scuttled, she is currently moored in dry dock at C-Gate 3 now bearing the identification of Quincy 4. Quincy 4 was scheduled to stop for a final photo opportunity and removal of the remaining computer software including the ships guidance squares and all other salvageable circuitry before heading on to its blazing end." He paused for effect then neatly turned a page over in front of him. "Now it seems the real Quincy 4 has not been heard from since its departure from C-Gate 2 several months ago. Giving those figures she should be within an estimated eight weeks from C-Gate 6. C-Gate 6 Ladies and Gentlemen is the point of no return." He looked dead on in to the camera. "Our extra planetary news drones made this discovery early morning yesterday when we realized Quincy 4's computer still had her sitting at C-Gate 3. Our producer managed to file a salvage order on The Sandra K. in hopes a search of the ship would turn up Kester Trewer's remains."

"Stupid fools," Roman Trewer mumbled under his breath. He'd been in seclusion now for almost four months taking care of his business by phone and electronic communications. As long as Kester's bio chip transmitted life, all he could do is wait, worry and wonder where his son was. It was no secret that Kester's life style was going to be part of his fall from office. His approval ratings were on a steady decline for the past year and a half. The writing was on the wall. The governor knew two things no one else on Earth or in space as far as that goes knew.

#1) he didn't have Kester removed or killed and
#2) he knew Kester was still alive.

Where? Was the question not only on his lips but on everyone else's lips too? He was playing a game of political chess and had no clue who he was playing it with. His son Kester was the King and it was up to him to keep him from Check Mate. He poured himself a strong drink and watched the rest of the GBC breaking news story.

Lowell Harding continued to spew on about The Sandra K., Quincy 4, the Governor and Kester, sensationalizing more and more with his every word. By the time he was finished with the report, Lowell had Kester dead and his father Governor Roman Trewer the main suspect.

"Let's go live to our GBC drone waiting at C-gate 3, please keep in mind there will be a few seconds delay due to the distance." He turned his chair towards a big screen to his left, folded his hands in his lap and waited for the image to appear.

Viewers watched as the GBC drone started to transmit an image of The Sandra K. It turned on bright spot lights, illuminating the ships name, then panned its camera to the door. An audible hiss belched out as the outer hatch opened. Two armed figures wearing protective suits entered the first hatch. The door closed behind them and the drone switched to a remote camera strategically placed on the first officer's helmet. You could see his arm reach out and push a red button just before the inside hatch opened.

"Ok, we're going in to The Sandra K. now. Speculation is Kester Trewer the infamous son of Governor Roman Trewer will be found inside."

The camera started to pan the inside of the ship.

"No sign of Kester yet." He continued. "The ship is in remarkable condition considering it's scheduled to be scuttled. Why would anyone want to scuttle such a majestic ship unless there was something out of sorts going on here?"

Lowell Harding was now living one of his worst on screen moments and he was about to find out how bad. He crackled the airwaves.

"Keep in mind Ladies and Gentlemen, The Sandra K fell victim to a nuclear gel spill, which is the reason she needs to be scuttled. It obviously appears our officers inside did not get that information before entering. Do not be alarmed for their safety, those suits will stop just about any element including large doses of nuclear fallout from ever reaching the person inside. Now it looks as if the officers are moving aft, looking for any sign of life or a body. As you can clearly see, they're opening all the closet doors, searching every corner....." The first office held up his hand, in a halt motion. The second officer closed in behind him to have a look.

Lowell perked up at that moment.

"Wait a minute!" He excitedly said. "Looks like we might have something." He leaned in as closely to the screen as his chair would allow him.

Then the officer waved his hand as if waving off a pesky mosquito pointing toward the front of the ship where all the cockpit and all the controls were located. They walked forward through the ship's common quarters via the main isle. Panning from left to right, looking at a series of plush seats with tables and viewing screens attached to each. All were empty. Once inside the cockpit, Lowell Harding would be redeemed. His going nowhere story finally took a direction. The two customs officers took a seat in the cockpit command chairs. Just as they both sat down, Prime Minister Barry Wells typed a command on his keypad.

Lowell Harding was just about to start apologizing to his viewers when a startled customs officer jumped up out of his seat.

"Something's happening here. Panel lights are starting to flicker and one of the officers is now motioning to the other to leave the ship. You see it live here first folks, exclusively on GBC. The entire dash just came to life, as well as the viewing screen. Let's see if I can get a word from the officer." He pushed a button on his console. "Hello? Can you hear me? This is Lowell Harding from GBC, we're live with our viewers. Can you hear me?"

There was a short burst of airwave static when a female voice came over the speakers.

"Yes Lowell I can hear you perfectly."

"Can you tell us what just happened?"

"Yes sir, it appears a launch sequence has been issued from somewhere on Earth. I'm not really sure where it was issued from though. I do have to report, there is no sign of any creature alive or dead on board this vessel. As far as we can tell, using visual and infrared scanning. Nothing alive as you just saw as we walked through. This ship is empty."

"Yes, we saw. I have a few more questions if you don't mind."

Lowell was cut off by the woman officer.

"Listen Mr. Harding I will be more than happy to answer any questions you have, however right now, my partner and I have seven minutes and counting to vacate the ship and reach a safe distance."

They turned and started to walk out. Lowell Harding was near panic, he pressed the studio mute button and started to scream at the exiting officers. "Leave my camera on board... just leave it, place it facing the control panel and leave it!" He was now standing, no one viewing could hear a word he was saying, however due to his animated state and flaring arms he raised a few curiosities.

"Leave the camera!" He continued to scream. His face now beet red. "TURN AROUND AND...LEAVE...THE...CAMERA," his voice could not be raised another decibel. She stopped just short of the door then turned around. Lowell held his breath as the officer walked back in to the cockpit. He watched as the camera was removed from her helmet like a ship bouncing on the waves. It was gently secured to the arm of the Captains command chair facing the screen which now read, "All systems green." Large numbers ticked away the countdown to departure. The female officer closed the outside door with just a few seconds before five minutes left, saluted Lowell Harding with an upturned middle finger and scampered back to the safety of inside C-Gate 3.

Roman Trewer watched, along with the other millions of global viewers as the departure ticked its way down to zero. There was only one place his son could be now and it was not on God's green Earth. He also knew now, that Kester was set up by Frank (Yoman) Lewis and Prime Minister Barry Wells. He could only hope and pray that since Kester's I.D. chip still showed signs of life that he was safe and in good health. He called his only trusted person and friend, his chauffeur William and thanked him for his silence and dedication, then asked him to ready a private transport. Destination, Prime Minister Barry Wells's office.

The two men arrived the next day unannounced in the early morning hours. Governor Trewer had diplomatic status and no one ever questioned the arrival of his transport as it came to a stop in sub level three of the Canadian Offices of Government. A guard, smartly dressed in his service blues greeted the Governor and his traveling companion.

"Good morning sir," he said as he opened the transport door. He looked across the seat to see Bill Moss and greeted him in the same friendly manner. "The Prime Minister is not due in the building until seven, may I suggest a fresh breakfast and a hot cup of coffee? You have about two hours to wait."

Governor Trewer wanted to verbally thrash the young guard by informing him he knew how much time he had to wait. But the young man was only doing his job.

"Perhaps we could just wait in the Prime Minister's office?"

"I'm sorry sir." The guard said motioning his hand to the café'. "This way please. The food is always fresh, the coffee is always fresher and hot. The best I can do for now is a nice warm meal on the house."

Surrendering Governor Trewer responded to the invitation. "That would be wonderful, please show us the way."

They were escorted to an empty cafeteria and within a minute a waiter placed a pot of coffee along with a plate of breakfast rolls in front of them then handed them each a menu.

"Eat up." The Governor told Bill. This will be the last meal either one of us will eat on Canadian soil again. And eat up they both did, ordering fresh fruit, three different types of sausage and a stack of pancakes each. The men snickered a little while they ate and paid no attention to the small crowd starting to gather around them for breakfast as well. A moment later the guard who greeted them at the landing dock reappeared. He obediently stood at attention until Governor Trewer acknowledged his presence.

" Yes son, how may I help you?" He asked.

"Begging the Governors pardon sir, I just wanted to inform you my duty shift will be over at 6:30. My replacement, unfortunately will be unable to escort you to Prime Minister Wells's office. I trust you know your way, sir."

"I do indeed corporal and once again thank you for your dedicated service, and breakfast was quite delicious." Governor Trewer expected a reply but the guard only smiled, crisply turned his back to them and marched away.

"How lucky is that." Bill said as he stuffed a bite of maple glazed flapjack in his mouth.

"I think the Gods are on our side this morning." The Governor answered back.

"How'd you get in my office?" A startled yet angry Prime Minister asked his uninvited guest. He turned his head just in time to see William Moss kick the door closed from behind it. He then positioned himself between the Prime Minister and his desk, which now had Governor Trewer sitting in it. He reached in his pocket for his phone but a strong hand grasped his arm and pulled it down to his side.

"I wouldn't do that if I were you sir," Bill said.

Barry Well's eyes grew large with anger. "How dare you show up here unannounced and wait for me in my office. I have every right to ..." He was cut off by Trewer.

"You think you have rights? By the time I'm finished here, the only rights you'll have is the right to fight like a man or take like a wuss when you become someone's prison girl." Roman stood up and started to walk towards Barry.

"I figured it out, Wells. You had Lewis toss my son in the garbage didn't you? It took me awhile to put it all in place, too many rumors turned into facts over the last seven months. I kept telling myself, nah, Wells is scum but he aint that bad. The more I thought about you, the more I came to realize, yeah you are that bad." He was now standing close enough to smell Wells coffee breath. He raised his voice. "That is my son, Wells. He might have had some bad times but none the less he is my son, my only son and despite his screw up and yes, I know he made some dandies, I still love him. I swear on my wife's memory...."

Wells cut him off. "You'll what? You'll call the cops? You'll call who? You my friend don't have a leg to stand on. You're just a pathetic washed up old fart who still believes he has a political career ahead of him, and nothing more. That son of yours destroyed both our careers and it was a piece of cake to get Lewis to do my dirty work. Right now Lewis is a well-paid vacationer on his way to points unknown in the galaxy. He resigned his job and disembarked Quincy 4 on C-Gate 4 and my guess is he'll never look back. Now as far as trying to pin anything on me, go ahead. I'm done too. Only for me it's kidney failure." He chuckled slightly then added, "you would think during this era of medical genius I could have been cured." He raised an eyebrow, "matter of fact, I should have been cured, you know what the doctors told me?" Not expecting an answer he carried on with a blank stare. "They told me that one in seven hundred million bodies reject artificial organs. If I had known this in advance, I would have at least compared tissue samples with Kester before I had him killed. Oh wait, that wouldn't have worked anyhow would it? His kidneys are probably shot." At that moment Governor Trewer's fist connected with Prime Minister Wells's lower jaw and sent the man stumbling backwards until the floor broke his fall.

Roman walked over, kicked Wells in the ribs and said. "He's not dead." He stood where Wells was laying, produced a chip scanner, scanned Wells and confirmed he would be dead in less than a year. It seemed the doctors waited too long trying to introduce artificial kidneys and now even a live transplant is out of the question. Roman looked up at Bill and without words the two men headed for the door.

"It's not gonna matter." Wells mumbled.

They kept walking.

Wells started to laugh and spurting blood from his mouth, said it again. "It's not gonna matter."

Roman and Bill stopped at the door, turned to see Prime Minister Wells now sitting up, leaning against the wall, holding his ribs. Blood dripping onto his white shirt.

"We not only Hackjacked Quincy 4 with The Sandra K. but we amped it early. All records of Quincy 4 have been erased. It does not exist anymore. People waiting for its final arrival at Gates 4 and 5 will just shrug their shoulders with contempt. That tug is on its way to the sun and no one will even know it's still carrying people." He wiped the back of his hand across his face, looked at all the blood, winced a little then spat a few droplets on the floor. Roman walked back over to him, leaned his head in and whispered through gritted teeth. "I hope your death is painful." He turned and walked out the door. William followed. Neither man bothered to look to see if anyone had followed nor did either one care. Just before they reached their launch berth, William stopped in his tracks.

"What is it?" Roman asked.

"I left my jacket, I'll be right back, don't leave without me," he said in jest, turned around and disappeared behind a wall.

As Roman approached his transport he froze in his tracks. The same guard that greeted him this morning was still on duty. The guard walked over. "Allow me to assist you sir." He opened Trewer's door and stood there silent, waiting on William to return. The two men never said a word to each other. William reappeared without a jacket, the guard went back to his post, and Trewer hit the power. The next morning it was reported that Canadian Prime Minister Barry Wells was found non responsive in his office, an apparent accidental fall. He died five weeks later from his injuries. His name was never spoken between the Governor and his good friend and loyal companion Bill Moss again.

Lisa Lark slowly studied Kester Trewer in amazement. Here was a man who somehow survived almost nine months in the confines of some of the worse filth known to mankind. On top of that, he was severely injured, malnourished and grossly dehydrated. She simply could not wrap her mind around his survival.

She began to keep a record of his vitals while rehydrating his body. She cleaned the maggots from his wound and examined it closely. Looking through the massive hole in Kester's chest which now encompassed his abdomen she could see his intestines, pretty much collapsed now from lack of digestion. She seriously doubted he would make it home alive. Her decision to hold off on contacting his father, was confirmed by the fact they had no working communications on board. Carefully she inserted a small compressed air cylinder in his lower intestine. Slowly releasing the pressure she guided the pocket of air with her forefinger and thumb. It took well over an hour but she managed to re-inflate his lower intestine this way.

Miller answered the knock on his door to find an exasperated Ms. Lark standing there. She reflected the look of a woman who had just seen a ghost.

"He died didn't he?" Miller asked as he opened the door to let Lisa in.

"No, he's not dead yet and don't ask me how. I've never seen anything like this in all my years. I mean for all intents and purposes he should have died months ago and yet here he is. His heart beat all of four times the last minute I monitored him. I have him on fluids and as soon as I can, he'll be placed in a state of deep freeze and I just pray he makes it." She turned to leave, after taking a few steps towards the door she then turned back around, running her hands up the back of her neck, she stood there, now looking like a confused child. "I mean he survived this long, right? There must be a reason."

Miller's face was expressionless as he held up a coffee pot with a look of offering on his face.

"How bout a cup? Take a moment to unwind."

"Oh you're a life saver," she said as she slowly turned three hundred and sixty degrees in Miller's room.

"I love what you did to the place." She said checking out the new paint job.

Miller just smiled. "Two hundred and sixty four days and counting on this tub, I had to find some way to stay sane."

She sat down at his desk. He could see she was visibly shaken up.

"I guess I should be grateful I can't contact his father yet." she managed to squeak out of her quivering voice. "I mean you should see this man, right? He defies everything natural and medical and I don't see him ever functioning in life proper again." She stood up and started to flay her arms about in some dramatic ballet. "That wound, for crying out loud, have you seen that wound?" She knew he hadn't seen it yet, and on the verge of a breakdown she just kept right on talking. She held her hands up and made a circle the size of her head. "It's this big, and it was full of maggots, and oh wait, you've not heard the best part yet, have you?!"

Miller just slowly shook his head no, and could not get a word in if his life depended on it.

"Here's the best part my friend. Those maggots kept it clean." Her voice went up and octave and about three hundred more decibels. "I can't freaking believe it. No infection, no gangrene, no excessive bleeding. And then there is that eye, I mean you have to see this man's eye. Oh yeah buddy, he's gonna lose that eye for sure."

Miller carefully approached the panic stricken woman and wrapped his arms around her. She buried her face in his shirt and just wept. Mumbling and bumbling on and on about Kester Trewer's eye. When she finally stopped whimpering, Miller sat her down in a chair and waited for her to compose herself.

"Do you have children Ms. Lark?" He asked.

"Yes I do, two sons twenty four and twenty five, why do you ask?"

"I have two sons too about the same age." He replied, handing her a pint of Navy-blue paint.

"What am I supposed to do with this?"

Miller just nodded towards a wall that had already been splashed with several other colors of paint.

"Seriously?" She inquired.

"You bet," He said. "I think everyone should experience the deliberate splashing of paint on a wall at least once in their life."

"Just that wall?" She asked with a wry grin on her face.

Miller moved his arms in a circle, then picked up a pint of pink paint and commenced to splash it on the walls, the floor, the bed, the mirror, Lisa followed suit. They spent half an hour throwing paint in every direction possible when all the sudden Lisa stopped and looked at the label on the can of orange paint in her hand.

"Hey wait a minute, this paint belongs to us. It says right here on the label. Property of Three Day Shuttle Company. How did you get it?"

"I have my secrets." He had a big smile on his face.

"Good answer," she replied and then dipped her fingers in the orange paint and spattered Miller with it before she emptied the can in an aggressive random way.

They both stood there admiring their work for a few seconds.

"Thank you Mr. Miller, I needed that cup of coffee. Wish me luck, I'm headed back to medical to check on our man."

"Right behind you." Thinking, *there is no point in telling his father anything, because none of us are getting out of this alive.*

The two reappeared on the main station of the ship to find the other three men frantically sending out messages into space. Houtt turned to look at them.

"I see you two been having fun."

There was no hiding the multitude of different colored paint they were both wearing.

"Long story," Miller said.

Lisa stepped forward and stuck her hand out to Shooster first. "Thank you so much for your help." Then she thanked Manetti likewise. Shooster had nothing to say at all, he turned his head away in disgust.

"I would like to say the pleasure was all mine," Manetti retorted then added. "But there was nothing pleasurable about it, and to be honest, there is a part of me looking forward to roasting alive so I don't have to carry those memories through a long life."

She turned back to Miller, "I could use a hand in sickbay." She quietly walked away.

"Be there as soon as I brief these guys."

"So is that our guy and is he alive?" Manetti queried.

The four men stood looking out the view window of Quincy 4 which was now almost an opaque color of green. The sun engulfed the screen, no one spoke for a good two or three minutes when finally Houtt spoke up. "What are we gonna do with him?"

"We have one hope of him surviving and that's to suspend him. Somehow she thinks we're still getting off this tub. I tried to tell her but she just won't hear it. What have you guys found?"

They dropped their faces.

"Nothing good," Manetti started. I've been sending coded messages through the emergency access channels. Switching from one channel to the next to the next. I don't even think the messages are getting out."

"I've been on the audio synth every minute blasting screeches out there in hopes someone will pick them up. Problem is we don't even know where we are now, so how is anyone else ever gonna find us?" Shooster said.

"And you Mr. Houtt, got any good news?"

"Nope, I've been sending S.O.S. and mayday every alternate minute with Shoe. Between the three of us, this ship is a nonstop beacon of despair. I imagine, we'll just sit here until we can no longer stand the heat, at that point we'll leave the kitchen and head for the pods." He turned and sat back down, picked up the microphone and continued with his fruitless cries for help.

"I'll be back up as soon as Kester's frozen. I'm gonna go give Lisa a hand."

"Judging by the looks of things you already have," Shooster mumbled just loud enough to be heard.

"Stow that crap Shoe, she's been traumatized too, and regardless of what you think about Miss happy hoo ha, she's here just like us till the end."

Shooster took a few huffed steps towards Miller, stuck his index finger out and pointed at him. "You haven't worked here long enough to talk to me like that you got it." His eyebrows were raised like an elephant would extend its ears just before it charged.

Miller turned and walked off the bridge without saying another word.

"How's your patient?" Miller asked as he entered sickbay.

"Again surprisingly, he seems to be making a slight improvement, and I mean slight. You ready to do this?"

Miller never put a person in suspended animation before, however he was well read on the subject. "You should know before we get started that the cat died."

Lisa knew exactly what he was talking about. In the academy everyone is given a live cat to place in suspended animation for a period of thirty days.

"More times than not, the cat dies," she said. "Let's get started."

"No time like present."

They carefully layered sheets of Skinthetics over the open wound, then wrapped him tight in a thin film resembling a plastic wrap membrane. They carried his body to a submersible tank apply dubbed a sarcophagus. His body weighed no more than eighty five pounds which was a problem in itself but there was no other option. They placed the body in the tank and inserted syringes into each arm and leg, then attached plastic tubing to each syringe.

"Vital signs please?" Lisa asked.

"Temperature 89.4F blood pressure 56 over 19 and heart beats 16 per minute." Miller delivered the stats professionally, even though in his mind he kept thinking this was a waste of time.

"Lower the mask," she ordered.

Miller removed a face mask from inside the would be tomb and secured it on Kester's face. Immediately oxygen started to be pumped into his lungs. His chest heaved up and down rapidly for a few seconds to insure proper re-inflation of his lungs before it fell into a nice steady rhythm.

"Totally amazing," he whispered.

"Tell me about it," Lisa exclaimed. "Ok we need to raise his body temp to normal and then drop it."

Miller knew the drill and figured she was just talking to hear herself and hoped if she did or said anything wrong he would correct her. One of the phenomenon involved in suspending anything alive was you had to start with whatever that creature's normal body temp is. In this case 98.6. It took a good hour for this to happen.

"Again I want to thank you for helping me out when I was about to break down," Lisa said to Miller.

"You know it's all good, to be honest, those other guys are cut from a different cloth, they look at my claustrophobia as a weakness and I suppose it is, but if anyone on board this death ride knows anything about freaking out it would be me. Your man here would have never been pulled out if it were left up to me."

She glanced up and tried to smile. "We all have a part to play in this, and I still don't buy it that we're on a death ride." She checked the stats. "Ok we're at normal temp, let's start with the femoral arteries first. Miller turned a knob and a clear liquid started to enter Kester's body forcing his blood to be pushed out through the exit tubes. Each time this cycled through his body temp dropped a few degrees and his veins and arteries became more pliable and more useful. From this point everything was automated, when his body reached 30.5 degrees the sarcophagus would close and seal itself.

"Our job is finished, how 'bout you and I go have a real word with our buddy Mr. Lewis and see about getting off this so called death ride."

"If you insist, but first I think, if we expect anyone to ever take us serious again we should get out of these paint spattered clothes."

She looked at Miller and then down at her own clothes. She never realized until now she looked like a Jackson Pollack painting. "Um good idea, meet outside Lewis's quarters in half an hour, and keep this to ourselves please, don't really want or need your fellow idiots getting in my way."

"Got it, I'll see you in half an hour."

They went in separate directions when Miller called after her.

"Hey!"

She looked over her shoulder at him, "yes?"

"Did you just call me an idiot?"

"I call it like I see it Mr. Miller." She said with a straight face.

"Alright then Miss happy hoo ha, see you in a half an hour."

"Touché," she said and disappeared around the bend of the ship.

The Sandra K. sat fully compressed alongside a small fleet of abandoned spacecraft destined to be either vaporized or auctioned off. C-Gate 3 security took no chances. Decompression of a launching ship was not to taken lightly. Even though there was no heat exchange, there was still enough exit thrust to propel a ship from here to the gravitational pull of the sun. A red light began to blink at the back of this ship. This was the twenty minute warning light, or the twenty minute light as it was called. Next there were small bursts of thrust from the side of the ship. With each small burst the ship moved a few yards into a better position for launch. The blinking red light began to blink faster indicating ten minutes until launch. A row of bright white lights clanked on illuminating the path in front of the ship. The blinking red light became a steady red light indicating five minutes until launch. The ship released small blasts of vapor from its many positioning ports just seconds after it was lifted off the ground by its belly thrusters. A small dust and debris cloud swirled out of its way and with a loud steady swooshing The Sandra K., electronically disguised as Quincy 4 jetted off to a destination unknown. (At least for now.)

Governor Trewer sat in silence, the chip implant in his son Kester stopped beeping back its signal. One of two things were possible. He either was dead or in suspended animation. His mind kept telling him what his heart didn't want to know. His son was dead. Bill Moss knocked on his door.

"Come on in Bill."

Bill had no words for his friend, he chose to sit in silence or at least until Roman spoke.

"A political career is a killer of all things sacred, you know that Bill? One day you're on the top of your game, then you spend the rest of the game lying, stealing, cheating and turning your back on those you love. There's no dignity left in my life. I sit here in a mansion I don't even own. I have a fleet of the most luxurious modes of transportation I don't even own. One of the world's most powerful men and yet I have nothing. When did this happen?" He asked a question that had no answer.

"I'm sorry Boss," Bill said.

"Please don't call me boss, Bill. You and I have been friends for a long time, you've been my eyes and ears all these years. I just always figured there would be a different end to it all."

"I have two pieces of business to tell you Roman and I'm afraid one of it is pretty bad news. First The Sandra K left Gate 3 about twenty minutes ago and secondly your favorite detective is waiting in the drawing room for you. He's got three other men with him. If you like I can ready a rail for you?"

"Naw no need for running, I'm innocent, you know that and I know that. Send em up, let's get this taken care of." While he waited he turned on the news just in time to watch footage of The Sandra K pull away from the news drone like a shot from a gun. He knew she was now compressed for speed, still unsure what it all meant though. "Chief Burns, please come in and have a seat, I was just watching more of my saga unfold here. How can I help you today?" He asked while pouring a cup of coffee. "Would you like some?"

"Thanks but no, we need to ask you to come in again and talk with us."

"Am I under arrest?"

"Good news is, that's hardly the case."

"And the bad news is?"

"We think we found your sons remains. They're pretty badly decomposed and I have to warn you it's not going to be easy."

"That's impossible, Burns. If my son is dead, he died today and his remains would not be decomposed at all yet."

"How do you know he died today?" The chief asked him while producing a small notebook and pen from his pocket. "You're not going to tell me you've been withholding important information are you.

"Up until this morning I've been protecting my position as a world leader, as you know I am exempt from most of the law and that doesn't mean I break them. I have set a lawful example to all the people and I won't stop now. So yes there is some information I will now give you. Kester had an implant chip, it beeped back the minimal vitals to this little device." He pulled a small black plastic object from his desk, then tossed it to Chief Burns. "As you can plainly see the last indication of his being alive via his vitals being sent to that device ended within the last twenty four hours."

"I'm sorry I bothered you sir, and I'm sorry for your loss." Just that quick Roman found himself alone again.

Miller met Lisa in front of the door to Frank Lewis's private quarters. The door opened and they both stepped inside.

"Is it time for my last meal?" Frank asked barely looking up.

Lisa walked in and positioned herself in front of Lewis. She reached out grabbed his scruffy beard and pulled his head up so his eyes met hers.

"Tell me how to get off this ship!" She demanded.

A big bad breathed grin came across Frank's face. "That's easy lady, no problem at all. You want off?"

"Yes," she answered knowing Frank was being condescending towards her, but could only manage that one word.

"Go to the airlock, push the red button and voila, you're off the ship."

She slapped him hard across his face, this caused Miller to approach them. Without looking behind her, she placed a hand on his chest and stopped him. She now had Miller by the chest and Lewis by the beard and no one moved.

"I need to know what you did and how to stop it."

"Aint gonna happen lady, I screwed up, I screwed up so badly I'm going down with you all and there aint a fricken thing any of us can do about it either."

She tightened her grip on his beard and Miller backed off her other hand and sat down.

"Explain it to me then, because no one gets lost in space these days... no one!"

"Ok then, you want an explanation, I'll give it to you. This ship is Hackjacked, her identity was replaced with The Sandra K, a class A mining cruiser. They turned her into a salvage ship then moth balled her at Gate 3. You see I was supposed to get off at Gate 3 when we dumped some software. But Noooo guess who had to show up unannounced? You! So we never stopped at Gate 3. At that point the system was over ridden to A.M.P., so basically we don't exist, or at least we didn't exist. I'm sure there is some news about us by now." He reached his hand to meet Lisa's and pulled it away from his beard. "Let me ask you a question. Do you have any idea of how vast space is? For anyone to find us before we fry will be entirely happenstance. We are smaller than a pea in the Pacific Ocean. When you showed up with your drone and took our cubes, well guess what? I was gonna dash remember? And before I was gonna dash, I switched the cubes. So now we have no communications coming in or going out. Try as you may but I replaced the communications cube with the redundant cube and that was A.M.P.'ed. It's completely empty. No memory of our mission, no memory of our cargo, heck it doesn't even remember us. So getting back to the airlock and the red button... might not be such a bad idea after all huh?"

Miller walked over, then broke three of his fingers laying Lewis out cold on his floor.

Lisa marched her way to the control bridge, a woman on a mission now. "Excuse me," she said to Houtt who was still sending signals and maydays into the nothingness. Houtt just looked at her with a surrendering gaze of disbelief and defeat in his eyes but said nothing. She turned to Shooster next. "I need a keyboard and I need one now!" She screamed at him.

"Hey by all means lady take it, sure as I'm sitting here, it's not doing me a bit of good." He relinquished his seat to her.

She frantically started punching numbers and passwords into the ships computer. The four men stood there quietly watching and listening to her talk to herself under her breath.

"No, this can't be happening. How does a ship get lost in this day and age?" She whispered to herself. One by one they quietly walked away and left her to her task. The only thing they had going for them was time. It would be at least another twenty days until the gravitational pull of the sun would naturally initiate perpetual acceleration at which point it would all be over.

The Sandra K. now following a faint signal from Quincy 4, a signal that was undetectable to anyone else due to the fact she was now linked to Quincy 4 through the Hackjack of their computers. It was part of the company's insurance policy that all ships incorporate this system. No insurance company wanted to pay out that kind of money when a ship became lost or Hackjacked. Quincy being old enough to have had this system installed it was nothing but dumb luck for the crew on board.

"I need everyone here on the bridge with me immediately." The ships intercom came to life with Lisa's beckoning. All four men met in the corridor just outside of her line of sight.

"What does she want now?" Manetti asked.

"Beats the beans out of me," Shooster retorted.

"Beats the beans out of you?" Manetti chuckled looking at his long time good friend.

Shooster just smiled, lifted his left leg slightly off the floor and ripped a fart.

"Thanks Shoe, I love you too," Manetti said while backing up a few steps.

Houtt and Miller were trying to peek around the corner to see what was going on. All they could see was Lisa sitting at the main computer terminal typing away like she was writing a novel. She turned to see if her colleagues were on their way when she caught Miller and Houtt peeking at her.

"Quickly," she said with a motioning of her hand. Then pointed to her screen. "Tell me what you make of this."

Miller was the first to close in on her, looking over her shoulder. "I see it."

"Put it on the big screen," Houtt suggested.

The massive 8x10 foot screen came to life and they all just stood there with their mouths opened.

"How did you find this?" Houtt asked.

"Well while you losers were giving up, I refused. Persistence is one of my strong points. According to what I have been able to get these sad excuses of computers to do, I managed to figure out the name of the ship we been jacked to. She's a class A mining cruiser called The Sandra K."

An image of the ship was brought up on the screen along with a list of all her owners and all her duties while she was in service.

According to this information it seems our guest on ice's father once had a stake in her. Now if this isn't a coincidence, then nothing is.

Shooster took a few steps towards the screen. "It's tracking us, right?"

"I would like to think she is, I mean I can't see any other reason for her to be out here other than trying to catch up to us."

"How far away is she"? Miller asked.

"My calculations, have her catching us in about seventeen days. That gives us a three day cushion before perpetual acceleration. Looks like she's traveling twenty times faster than we are, I hope she can stop in time to pick us up." Lisa said jokingly then added, "I want twenty four hour eyes on this screen. I'll take the first shift, Miller you're next, then Shooster, Manetti and you Mr. Houtt." She said twisting her head around her shoulders making eye contact with them all.

On Earth the saga was being played on worldwide communications. Every reporter and broadcast company now had its own speculative story going on. The one thing the other stations did not have however was a camera neatly placed inside The Sandra K.

The camera was strategically positioned to view the big screen on the ship. It transmitted back to Earth, her location, her speed and every other important shipboard information. Most notably though she was equipped with a pretty new version of a Lazar system.

Being broadcast in to every living room of every home, every office and every coffee shop twenty four hours a day seven days a week was the sweeping arm of the Lazar system and the steady beep of contact with the lost tug and garbage barge. The Sandra K was the only vessel remotely offering a glimmer of hope to catch Quincy, and that glimmer was as distant as distance could be. Nonetheless every eye around the world was now tuned into GBC news.

"What about eyes in the sky? We got anything out there?"

"I'll call the guys, we'll go over our notes and see what we can come up with," Millie said as she stood up to walk out the door. She stopped. She turned around slowly.

Paul Downing looked up at her. "What?"

"Remember when the Miners Union had that trouble on Gate 5? What was it? Something to do with rights to claims and claim jumping. That ditzy red head you thought was hot did the story." She strategically placed a thoughtful finger on her chin. "What is her name?"

"You mean the current Mrs. Downing?"

"Yes! That's the one, and how is Hagatha doing?"

"Be nice. So I don't always make the right decision, your relationships are nothing to write home about either."

"Touché boss, but my point is we have surveillance at Gate 5."

He looked at her puzzled.

"Um surveillance drone, I forget which number, you sent all the way out there. Remember? For a story that had been dead weeks before it got there. Remember? Decided it would cost more than it was worth to bring it back. Remember? And you still married the red head even after corporate told you to fire her. Remember?"

"Yeah, yeah, yeah I remember and I know what you're getting at. Who's at Gate 5 we can depend on?"

"Well let's see now."

She started to walk in a circle. "Hmmm Gate 5, we have hardened miners and criminals hiding out there. We have prostitutes who will never be allowed back on Earth there. We have…." She was stopped by her boss.

"Ok Millie I get it… now it's your job to find me someone who can power up that drone." He said as he held his office door open, signifying it was time for her to get to work.

She smiled on her way out and said, "Give my best to Hagatha for me."

Just before he closed his door, he called after her, "And Millie?"

She turned around.

"At any cost, right. We need to keep this story fresh."

She saluted him and went to work.

Later that week Paul Downing's phone woke him from a sound sleep.

"I found your man on Gate 5 and he assured me our drone will be launched within the next three hours. Got a pen?" Millie asked.

A groggy voice said, "Hold on a second."

Almost a minute passed before he came back to the phone. "Ok what you got?"

"Here are the input numbers, these should give us exclusive access to all transmissions and video broadcast back." She rattled off a series of numbers. He repeated them back to her then hung up the phone. Millie finally went back to bed and Paul was forced to give up his sleep now that his adrenalin was pumping with excitement. He quickly punched those numbers in his computer and immediately a fuzzy screen popped up. All he could do now was wait for the transmissions to start.

On a normal commercial trek from Earth to C-Gate 6 it would take about fifty six weeks. This was including stops along the way respectfully from gates 2 through 5. Most trips usually stopped for reasons better left unsaid on the way out and hightailed it home on the way back. A non-stop commercial trek to gate 6 usually took about fifty weeks. A non–stop trek at intercept speed took only 22 weeks. The Sandra K.
now traveling at intercept speed was due to catch Quincy 4 just under three weeks before the tug entered perpetual acceleration into the sun. With a stroke of luck for the news station, the drone that just left C-Gate 5 was scheduled to catch up to both ships at about the same time.

4 Weeks to C-Gate 6

There was finally a visible blip on Quincy's radar screen. Estimated time for external camera visual was three weeks.

Miller happened to be the one on watch when a faint bright dot visibly appeared on the screen. He didn't see any reason to alarm anyone, it would be another three weeks before it would be close enough to help them. By the time Shooster took watch, Lisa joined him on the bridge.

"Why didn't you wake me up when you had visual of The Sandra K?" She snorted like a wild boar at Miller.

"Why would I?"

"Don't you think this is important?"

He could tell she was looking for an argument. "Well I figure we need to stay sharp and this time next week, none of us will be sleeping. I won't let it happen again." He said with a stupid smile on his face.

The blip on the radar showed a rapid approaching green dot, even if it was over a hundred and twenty five thousand miles behind them. At this speed there was no doubt it would catch up to them. The bleep on the screen became a hypnotic metronome as long as it stayed steady. It represented some type of perverted sense of security. As the days passed with The Sandra K looming behind the ship, those on board started to concentrate more on themselves. Shooster was sitting at the controls nodding off when the green blip on the screen became two. Beep beep, beep beep, he first opened one eye to make sure he wasn't dreaming. He glanced at the screen and saw there was another blip. Quincy 4 was refitted with a lazar (laser/radar) some fifty years ago. At that time it was state of the art equipment. Its range was as infinite as a light beam but the screen would only detect one hundred and fifty thousand mile radius. Whatever it was, it too was traveling at intercept speed.

The live broadcast from inside The Sandra K was fixed on her visual screen. Not much to see really. A circular image with a green dot in the center which represented Quincy 4. The day and time clicked away in the lower left corner and that was about it. Still it kept the world glued to their screens and the company was loving it. The drone from gate 5 however, was a different story. Equipped with cameras and filters once it was within

Quincy's parameters it would give the world a live video feed. Paul Downing and his crew were about to win a Pulitzer Prize for reporting.

3 Weeks

Lisa sat intensely on the bridge watching the mystery unfold of the second blip on their screen. She increased the power on the ships camera pointed behind them. She could make out The Sandra K but still all she had on the second blip was… it was a second blip. Lewis was sitting in his berth watching his screen in disbelief. This marked the second circumstance he didn't plan for. Again he thought he had all his bases covered and again he was wrong. He never thought the Hackjacked computer would be connected to the ship somehow. But it was. Then again he never really knew the history behind The Sandra K. Just then his intercom came to life. It was Houtt.

"Hey Frank, I know you're watching all this unfold but don't get your hopes up buddy. You aint getting rescued with the rest of us. I'll personally see to it. Do you know what the survival record is for anyone returning after passing by C-Gate 6?"

Frank knew the story. It was called the miracle at Gate 6. The story was about the mining ship Diamond Star being where it wasn't supposed to be. Perpetual acceleration put her four days past C-Gate 6 and by the time the crew figured it out all they could do was try to reverse their direction and by some miracle The Diamond Star and its crew made it home safely.

"Four days Houtt, yeah I know what the record is."

"I'll be nice to you though, just before I disembark, I'll slide your key under your door, at least you can wander the ship before you fry." With that Houtt turned his intercom off and missed all the kind words Frank had to say about him and where he could stick his rescue.

2 weeks

The blips on the radar screen now melted into one, whatever was behind The Sandra K, it was now close enough not to be detected.

Manetti was convinced to a man it was military and it was going to destroy The Sandra K. He'd been in seclusion for a few days. Every time he ate he couldn't keep his food down. His hands were visibly shaking and he was losing weight. Shooster tried talking to him, but to no avail. Miller knew better as did Lisa. But Houtt wouldn't take rejection as an answer.

"Open the door Vince, we need to talk."

There was no response. Houtt banged on the door a few more times.

"If you don't open this door so we can talk, I'll use the master, one way or another we're gonna talk."

Finally Manetti opened the door to let him in. "They're gonna blow it up aren't they?" he asked Houtt.

"I have no idea Vince, but why else would they send it so fast. I would also venture to guess The Sandra K is empty. There's not soul one on board that ship. If it's not a rescue ship someone somewhere knows why. I've been beating my head against the wall trying to figure it all out. We have Kester Trewer on board this ship in suspended animation. That tells me either his dad wants him home alive or he wants us all dead."

Manetti sat down on the edge of his bed, sunk his head in his hands and just rubbed his bald head front to back repeatedly. He looked up at Houtt. "I have been trying to raise both ships from my quarters, no acknowledgement whatsoever."

He turned on his communications screen, both men stood there staring at it.

"It just makes no sense, why would there be two unmanned ships sent out to us unless one of them was a missile."

"This mission was doomed from the beginning." Miller's voice was heard from the doorway. "It's all politics. We were never supposed to return, that's my take on this whole mess."

Just in the short time the three men stood there talking The Sandra K inched closer to them.

"If we could only see behind her." Miller whispered. "If we could only see behind her."

The news feed kept running twenty four hours a day non-stop. You could now see a clear image of The Sandra K from less than two hundred feet. With every hour that passed the mammoth barge became bigger as well. Within a weeks' time the rear of the barge dwarfed both The Sandra K and the drone. Everything looked intact and normal from this vantage point…as it should. This distance in space there was a twenty two second delay back to Earth. Those who were following this saga on Gates 4 and 5 were watching in real time.

Lisa sat in the main chair on the bridge with Shooster next to her. "I wish I could see the ship behind The Sandra K." She said under her breath.

Shooster stood up and walked over to another control panel across the room. He was putting in commands and programs then switched the image on the main communications screen.

"Well I'll be…" He heard Lisa say, just before she called the other men to the bridge.

She looked over her shoulder at Shooster with a nod and a smile.

"Oh we got all kinds of cameras attached to us lady. We got cameras on top, on the bottom, on both sides, all you had to do was ask."

Shooster then extended the camera on top another three hundred feet up, then angled it down by thirty degrees and as plain as day everyone was looking at The Sandra K *and* the drone that was following her.

"It's a news drone!" What the heck is a news drone doing out here and how did it get here?" He said.

Houtt stood there with his arm around Manetti's shoulder while Miller took the empty seat on the other side of Lisa.

"Did you know about theses cameras?" Manetti asked him.

"Not my job, I'm not involved." Houtt answered him with Shooster's favorite answer. He then hollered over to Shooster. "Hey Shoe, why didn't you tell us this weeks ago?"

"No one asked weeks ago, never dawned on me until just now. I'm like … Hey! We got cameras all over the place. I'm the sweep remember? It's my job to know these things. We got cameras on the sides, on the bottom and on the top. I can point them at anything you want to see. Want to see Saturn, no problem." He punched in a few codes and an image of Saturn popped up.

All Lisa could think is, *"what a moron. With that type of hardware on board and he waits until now to show us."*

"What about Gate 6 Shoe?" She asked him. "Can you zoom in on that too?"

"Sure if I knew where we are I could. Problem is we got nothing as far as navigation. If we hadn't A.M.P.'ed I could follow our trajectory but without our computer, for all I know we could be a million miles away, and as far as that goes we might just plow right into it too. I can tell you this, there is no blip on our radar so we're at least a hundred and fifty thousand and one miles out."

The Sandra K was close enough now to make out her ID numbers with the use of the camera zoomed in.

"She should be slowing down soon to match our speed. Another six days and we're going home… I hope," Houtt said before retiring to his berth.

Once inside his quarters, he opened the satchel that contained his personal belongings. He sat quiet and went through his wedding album page by page. Pictures that now only stood for bad memories. His divorce papers, were still sealed. He knew by the time he made it back to Earth there would be nothing left for him to go home to anyway. He held up the bottle of champagne he brought with him, stuck a cigar in his mouth just to get a taste of the tobacco, chewed the end a bit then placed it in his shirt pocket. He brought one for everybody on board. With his wry sense of humor, he wondered if he should give Lewis's to him as a warped joke or if Lisa liked the taste of cigars. In the back of his mind he knew he wasn't going to give it to Frank. Next in his bag were the pictures of his children, by the time he gets home they'll be two years older and even though they were now both grown into young adult men, he still felt lonely and sad that he missed two of their birthdays. He turned on his personal recorder and sent them each another message, something he'd been doing daily since he left Earth even though he knew for the last twenty some weeks his messages were only being broadcast into the cold nothingness of space. His last transmission for the day was to his now ex-wife. He called her every name in the book and wished she would end up with ptomaine poisoning and be painfully sick before she died. He felt a little better, closed his eyes then dozed off.

The following day, nothing changed. The Sandra K and the drone were still gaining on them with no sign of either one slowing down to match their speed.

The people on Earth were mixed over the rescue mission. For the most part people were rooting for a clean rescue. There were those though protesters who still wished ill fate on the entire mission. The crew of Quincy 4 were regarded as criminals in some sectors of civilization. The persistent dumping of trash in space divided the masses since its inception and maiden flight some hundred and fifty years ago.

From the camera on the drone the barge now filled the entire screen, you could read the company name and logo as big and bright as day. The vast barge sheltered both The Sandra K and the drone from growing heat and sun light now, they were safely tucked in behind it.

Mille, Buck and Franz sat in the studio operations room wondering the same thing. Why hasn't the Sandra K started to slow down? If she strikes the back of the barge she would surely cause a catastrophic disaster. That would definitely be the story of the millennium.

"Should we spin that?" Buck asked his two cohorts.

"We would own the airwaves at least for another five days if not longer," Franz added.

"Step ahead of you guys," Millie said from across the room where she was trying to get ahold of her boss.

Paul Downing was more than agreeable to his reporters desire to run with the story speculating what The Sandra K was doing by not slowing down and what would happen if she did plow into the back of that barge. Thousands of tons of garbage scattered into space just days before perpetual acceleration? Some of the bigger pieces would probably continue until they fried but all that smaller garbage would just sit there…forever.

A couple hours later the three reporters were sitting in Paul Downing's office.

"Ok this is the new story," Millie started.

"We have one tug and barge, not just any old tug and barge but Quincy 4, the last of the tugs built on Earth then assembled in space. We have a phantom ship The Sandra K…" Paul stopped her there. "Phantom ship, I love it."

"That was mine." Franz spoke up.

Millie cast him a sideways smile then continued.

"We have a phantom ship The Sandra K hot in pursuit and as of yet no sign of slowing down or changing course. And that puts her on a collision course. We have our drone tucked in right behind The Sandra K and also destined to collide barring the same issues. We have the potential makings of an epic disaster, one which will further divide our planet on the issue of space dumping. Now all we need is the streets filled with protestors and I could smell a Pulitzer Prize."

"Very nice work, you'll have my recommendations for that Pulitzer with or without protestors in the streets, but if this is anything like the protests of the past, give em time, they'll be out soon.

1 week

The Sandra K and her drone shadow now moved so close to the rear of the barge, Shooster had to readjust the camera angles again. This time it was set at a forty eight degree angle. They were literally looking down on top of the two ships now. The pair were now just one hundred miles out and closing fast. Everyone on board once again feared for the worse. There was going to be a collision and it was going to happen in the next three hours.

Lisa started to pace the floor while keeping an eye on the large screen.

She turned to Manetti. "When they hit us will it destroy both the barge and our ship?"

"Depends on just how fast they hit us and where they hit us I suppose. Doesn't really matter at this point though does it? How can something so simple end up so messed up? We have about three hours lady, I don't know about you but I'm gonna go send messages back to my loved ones and have a long talk with the man upstairs." He left her to pace the floor.

Miller was in his quarters spending the last of the paint and jamming to his favorite music as loud as he could get it. It resonated through his door and down the corridors to the bridge. No one was going to say a word. He stood in the center of the room with six different colors of cans of paint open in front of him. Like a classical music maestro he would dip his hands in one color and splash it across the room. Then another color and splash it up on the ceiling then the floor until he worked himself up in a crescendo of madness spinning in a circle whipping paint on everything until all he had left was one can of black enamel. He convinced himself he finally lost it. He sat down in the multi colored puddles of paint in the center of the room and recorded his final goodbyes to his friends and family. Stepping though the red, blue, yellow and green paint on his floor, he tracked it to the bridge where he was standing with the last can of black enamel and a paint brush in his hand. Without saying a word he walked up the large screen which now showed the nose of The Sandra K within striking distance and in big bold black letters he painted the name *Icarus* right smack dab in the middle of the screen, tossed the can and brush down on the floor and plopped into the center command chair to wait for impact.

Shooster being a couple feathers light of a pound still didn't realize he was about to be vaporized and not by the sun but by the cold expanse of infinite space, just sat there saying. "She's getting closer and closer now." This went on for a good half hour. No one said a word to him, mostly they just felt sorry for the man. Black paint was running down the screen when he switched cameras from the back to the portside view. "Hey wadda ya know, she's going around us." He said with his Shooster chuckle. He never really cared for Miller since day one but since it was just the two of them on the bridge at that moment he spoke again. "Take a look," he said and pointed to the screen. Miller looked over and sure enough, the port side camera showed The Sandra K moved over far enough to go around the barge.

Lisa who had succumbed to the fact this was her final moments in life was watching on the screen in sickbay which now became her quarters. She stood up awestruck, her jaw opened and watched as The Sandra K gracefully started to pull alongside of them. "Now what?" She whispered not realizing Houtt had entered her quarters unannounced.

"Yeah, I was watching it too in my room, you're a corporate honcho what do you make of this?"

She just stood there shaking her head. "I have no idea what to make of this, she's seems to be going too fast to rescue us though that's for sure. And that drone stayed right behind her?" She asked already knowing the answer.

"Yep, right in her shadow, some turn of events this turned out to be. I'll meet you on the bridge." He turned to leave, "Hey what did you do with our friend Kester?"

"Oh, since I had to stay in here, I thought it was kind of creepy to have him lingering about so I rolled him down to the donuts. I figure it's the farthest point away from the sun and I can get dressed and undressed without the feeling of being watched. I put him in donut number two, just in case you want to say goodbye." She didn't mean for that last statement to sound so horrible but she couldn't take it back now either.

"More like thank him is the right thing to say, I still believe if it weren't for him, we wouldn't be here now. See ya on the bridge."

The five of them stood on the bridge looking at a giant screen with the name Icarus painted in big bold black letters across it. Miller was standing there with every color of the rainbow stuck to him including some black enamel.

"Nice work." Manetti leaned over and whispered in his ear.

Houtt had nothing to say but could not keep the smile off his face either.

Shooster was trying to figure out what the word was and what it meant, when Lisa spoke up.

"I could have you fired for this." Her anger momentarily took the place of her common sense and by the time she figured that out it was too late, even she broke out in a frightened laughter.

Miller started to laugh too, it was a small slow chuckle at first but it began to pick up steam as he thought more about what she just said. Now he was completely out of control laughing a real belly laugh, snorting through his nose and spattering droplets of spittle in all directions. "Fire me? Oh please by all means just fire me. Does that mean I can get off this thing before we die? Hey I got it, how about I just do what Frank suggested and go push the red button! The cold vacuum of space sounds better than frying like an egg to me anyhow."

He started to leave the bridge but Houtt grabbed his arm. "You're staying right here with the rest of us Picasso. We aint dead yet and until we know for sure that ship and that drone have some way of pulling off a miracle, no one pushes the red button … got it?"

Miller said nothing and collapsed in a chair.

"Get me something to clean that screen with," Lisa bellowed.

"Its enamel." Miller said in a low monotone voice. "It aint gonna come off… my bad."

None the less the five of them sat there and watched the port side viewing camera as The Sandra K silently pulled alongside of them and started to pass. It took her almost three hours to completely breech them and an additional hour and a half for the drone to follow suit. They turned to face the front observation window which was now eighty five percent opaque and watched off to the left as the two ships started to pull away. Within a few hours everyone was now positive their last hope for rescue just whizzed passed them.

Houtt and Manetti became unwelcomed guests in Frank Lewis's quarters again.

"Not so tough now are you guys? Lewis said.

"What just happened Frank?" Manetti asked.

"Are you guys really this stupid? The Sandra "thinks" its Quincy, it wasn't sent here to save us. It's on a mission, a trajectory to the sun and the drone? Mystery to me too, never saw it before and don't know who owns it. You see, the ship we're on is derelict now, has been for months. We been going straight, sort of, only because we have the weight of the barge pushing us. We'll just float around in oblivion for a few more weeks then the sun will grab us and pull us in. If we're lucky, the sooner the better because I don't know about you two but I'm kind of tired of waiting on my fate. I would like to say it's been a pleasure flying with you boys but that would be a lie. Please close the door on your way out." And with that Frank turned his back to the two men and never saw them alive again.

Six days later there were two faint fiery lights in front of Quincy 4 everyone knew it was The Sandra K and the drone. It would be another week at perpetual acceleration and those two fiery lights will simply flash bright and vaporize, this will be there fate as well. At best they have six days left.

The temperature inside Quincy 4 was noticeably warmer the last two days. Miller moved out of his quarters and was holed up in donut number five. There was everything one person needed to survive up to sixty days inside the donut. He opened up communications to the bridge to follow the conversation. Like Lisa said about Kester, this is the farthest spot from the sun and his human instincts of survival forced him there. He figured if he had to, he could always put on his protective emergency suit that might buy him another twenty four hours.

Houtt grabbed his bottle of Champagne and his cigars and followed Miller's lead too. He was still sending messages out into the cold empty infinity in hopes that someone somewhere would intercept them and relay them back to Earth and his family.

Shooster, Manetti and Lisa stayed on the bridge despite the rising temperatures until The Sandra K and the drone poofed into vapor. By now they were wearing heat soles on their shoes and heat gloves on their hands. You could not touch any of the instruments without being mildly burned and the soles of their shoes were starting to leave marks melted onto the floor.

"Well I guess this is it my friend." Manetti turned to Shooster and shook his hand.

"I'll be seeing you when we get there." Shoe answered him.

All Manetti could do was think. *"We're here now buddy ole boy, we're here now."*

Neither man said a word to Lisa nor did she ever feel more alone than right now. Almost a year away from home and no way to even say goodbye. Chances are her children would never know what happened to their mother. Silently she locked herself in donut number 2 with the frozen body of Kester Trewer, the son of one of the most powerful men on Earth and it meant absolutely nothing.

The front of the ship outside was just starting to glow red when Shooster and Manetti locked themselves in donuts three and four. Communications channels were open to all five donuts but no one was saying a word until Houtt spoke. If I could get everyone to step out their donuts I would like to share a final moment with you all. The five of them looked at each other since their donuts were all facing inward in a circle. Lisa was the first one to cautiously step out and join Houtt on the landing, then Manetti, Shooster and finally Miller joined them too. Still covered in paint, he couldn't hide his shaking hands.

Houtt handed each one of his fellow travelers a hydro grown tobacco cigar. "The finest cigar in the known universe," he said, as he passed them out. He then held up his lighter, lit his and offered a light to everyone else. He then produced his bottle of champagne and five disposable drinking containers from his donut. He poured as close to equal amounts as he could in each container then tipped the bottle up and chugged the remainder by himself, flung it with all his might and they all watched it explode against the wall.

"I didn't envision the end of my life to unfold as it did during this mission." He held his drinking container up. "A toast to my fellow travelers, may our end come swift and painless and when our loved ones remember us, they remember the laughs and the love."

"Here, here." They all said in unison, clunked their containers together and took a sip.

He continued. "Shoe you've been a good friend for many years, thank you for the good times we spent up north. Vince we didn't always see eye to eye and there were times I just wanted to lay you out, but figured I would end up being the one on the floor, it was an honor serving with you too. Miller, I'm sure if we had had more time, I could have grown to like you too, just kidding man. God speed to you. Lady..." He raised his container to Lisa now. "Sorry we got off on the wrong foot..." The ship started to shutter and Lisa broke down hysterically bawling. Houtt put his arm around her gently and escorted her back her donut. He slapped the door button on the inside panel and got his arm out of the way just before her door closed and sealed her shut. She looked up at him but could not manage any other expression than sorrow. He turned to his mates. "See you guys on the other side." Shook their hands, dropped his cigar and stomped it out. Shooster, Manetti and Miller followed suit and within a minute all five of them were back in their donuts and sealed in.

Francis Baines Lewis was laying in his berth when the ship started to shutter and vibrate steadily. The dirty dishes and personal items he had laying around began to fall and hit the floor. Plastic started to melt all around him. Water lines began to leak and burst open spraying boiling water across the heated expanse of his room. The electrical started popping and shooting sparks like a fountain of fireworks.

He leaned his head back, cleared his thoughts and let his mind drift to a simple time in life. He could see himself as a young boy during a happier time. His mother was there, dressed beautifully, bringing a pitcher of lemonade from the house to a table set up outside. His father was grilling steaks on the grill. One of the rare times his family actually functioned as a family. He could taste the lemonade and smell the sizzle of the steaks. He opened his eyes and looked down and watched as the blood from his slit wrists dropped on the floor and started to sizzle, the smoke wafted up to his nose then everything faded to white.

The ship was violently shaking, instinctively everyone buckled themselves in. They could see all the plastic and lighter particle composites start to melt and drip. Fire extinguishers blew off their valves and started to spray white foam straight up in the air, it looked like something you would find at a party. Small fires started to break out as the flammable materials reached a point of ignition. Smoke could be seen but not smelled since they were all sealed tight inside their escape donuts safe from the disintegrating ship at least for another few minutes. They could see the ship twisting and cracking before their eyes, bouncing violently like an offbeat rhythm to some unintelligible fusion jazz song. Lisa tightened her belt and all the time she was doing this she was wondering why.

Manetti could be seen yelling and shaking his fist in anger.

Shooster was holding tight to the arms of his chair, he wet himself.

Houtt just sat there bouncing up and down with a look of terror on his face.

Miller was praying when the back of the ship opened up and the front of the barge became visible. None of them noticed it was the escape hatch doors opening. They all thought the ship finally broke apart. Disoriented as their donuts thudded against the barge, they rolled and tumbled alongside the barge, bouncing into it periodically causing more rolling and disorientation.

Although the violent shaking and bouncing came to an end, the five donuts continued to bang loudly into the side of the barge for another good twenty minutes until finally there was quiet and calm on the other side of the barge. They were now scattered and alone, floating in space as Quincy 4 and its last massive cargo of Earth's garbage began to glow a brighter red off in the distance.

Manetti's donut was the first, then one by one the remaining donuts followed. First the soft blue lights of the instrument panel lit up. Then the medical board lit up broadcasting his vital signs on the plastic screen in front of him. After that a red warning started to flash on the screen telling him his umbilical cord from his suit to his ship was not secure, so he plugged it in. Within a matter of seconds he could feel the suit tighten up on his body and start pumping warm fluid through the small tubes that were intertwined throughout it. They called them veins. He flipped a toggle switch to his left and spoke. "Houtt are you up and running in your donut?"

"Yep," he said with a slight upbeat in his tone.

"Same here," Miller chirped.

"Me too," said Lisa.

"Yep I got full power and life support here too," Shooster informed them.

The five donuts were scattered every which way when they bounced off the barge and were now several miles apart when they stopped tumbling and up righted themselves. Starting as tiny pinpoints in the distance the occupants of the donuts started to see one another. Slowly the pin points became larger and within a couple of hours they could make out who was in which donut.

"Lisa how's your passenger?" Houtt asked.

"I plugged him in to the medical panel, all I can tell you is, he's exactly the same as when I put him in here. So, for what's that worth, that's the only answer I have for you."

Manetti and Miller were the first two donuts to dock together, the two ships becoming one. Houtt docked with Shooster an hour later. They were still a short distance from Miller and Manetti when Lisa's donut made a maneuver to be included in the docking process and connected to Miller and Manetti, within the next hour Houtt and Shooster docked to the other three. As designed the two outside ships slowly powered themselves to dock with each other thus forming a complete circle with all the crew facing inward toward each other, hence making a donut formation.

"Any idea where we are and where we're headed?" Lisa asked.

The center of the circle of their donut lit up with a transparent hologram of the solar system.

"The small blue dot is us, the larger blue dot is Quincy 4. As you can see shortly it will no longer exist. But it looks to me we're just outside radar scope of Gate 6 so that's the good news. Bad news is we have no idea if anyone there can even rescue us. At our current velocity we should be in radar contact with them in about seven weeks." Houtt said.

We really ended up quite a ways off the beaten path, didn't we?" Lisa added.

"Could be worse, take a look." Houtt pointed to his left.

The seats inside the donuts swiveled forty five degrees so now everyone was facing the sun. There was a red streak with a long tail in front of them then a bright flash that spread like the explosion of a sky rocket trailing off into a puff of vapor. The grand old ship Quincy 4 and her final load of Earth's refuse was nothing but a memory now.

"So anyone have any theories of how this happened?" Miller asked.

"Act of divine providence?" Lisa said

"Doesn't matter to me, as long as we get home." Manetti said

"As far as I know, we should be a puff of smoke right now." Houtt chimed in.

"I know." Said Shooster. "It was Frank who saved us."

They all looked at him, waiting to hear what he had to say.

"Go on," Miller said, "do tell."

"Of course this is just my thoughts, I don't know for sure. When miss happy hoo ha here docked with us and we loaded the cubes on board that drone, who all was there?"

Lisa spoke first. "The name is Lisa, Mr. Shooster."

Shoe just waved her off dismissively.

"It was you, me and Lewis," Manetti said.

"Right and then you left, leaving only me and Frank. Then Frank persuaded me to let him load them by himself which was fine by me. Then he switched out our tracking and communications cube and replaced it with the escape donut cube. We had a way off that death ride the whole time and never realized it."

Just then Houtt chimed in." Our distress signal is being answered, quiet!" He turned up the volume on the inner communications system.

"This is the search and rescue ship Stellar Star 1, can you pick up this transmission?" A man's voice was crackling through.

"This is Jim Houtt electrical and communications officer of Quincy 4, and yes we are receiving this transmission."

"This is Captain Cale Morris on board search and rescue vessel Stellar Star 1 we have honed in on your distress signal, how many souls on board?"

"We have five conscious and one in animation and lost one crew member." Houtt relayed the information back.

"Well today is your lucky day folks, we just happened to be returning from a deep space exercise and picked up your signal. Can you elaborate on your status and provisions?"

"We have four members of the crew, one private law enforcement agent and one beyond critical in suspended animation. For the most part everyone on board is in good physical health. As far as provision go, we have enough to last us another thirty five days. We've been adrift now for fifteen."

"Roger that Quincy we are the closest ship to you, but still a good twenty one days out. Think you can hold out until then?"

"Piece of cake, Stellar Star1, we have you on our radar and we'll see you when you get here. This is the surviving crew members of Quincy 4 and guests signing out for now.

Epilogue

It took just under a year before the crew set foot on Terra Firma again. They came home to awards, accolades and a great big fat check, enough to more than retire comfortably on.

Vincent Manetti found a nice little cabin on sixteen acres of land with a great fishing stream cutting right through the middle. He had grown to respect the men he worked with on that ill-fated mission but couldn't care less if he ever saw any of them again.

Shooster and Houtt bought a lodge in the Upper Peninsula of Michigan and enjoyed sharing the tasks of hosting the vacationing families as well as the sportsmen. They both enjoyed long winter months riding snow machines and ice fishing. Jim Houtt died of liver failure at age fifty six, Shooster continued to run the lodge with his wife and daughter living to a ripe old age of ninety nine.

Miller and Lisa married and spent the next several years of their lives back in space. Lisa as an insurance fraud agent and Miller as a technical engineer specializing in anti-theft and Hackjacked systems. He developed and designed a program to interconnect all traffic in space by the mandatory installation of transponders on all commercial vehicles. They literally turned every commercial vehicle into a tracking satellite allowing any commercial ship to be tracked anywhere in the known galaxy. He named it The Icarus System.

Kester Trewer made a painfully slow recovery and after years of a strained relationship with his father, he moved to the Bahamas where he lived out the rest of his life clean, sober and incommunicado with everyone and everything from his past...including his father.

Roman Trewer was investigated heavily for criminal activities while serving office. These included, theft, bribery, extortion and murder. He was acquitted and re-elected to his position for three more consecutive terms before dying heart broken, bitter and old while sitting at his desk.

Garbage continued to be sent to the sun and people continued to be divided on the safety and moral issues of space dumping. The industrial moguls behind it continued to be perversely rich and deadly determined to stay that way.

Contact Dutch Fisher at dutchfisher33@gmail.com

Made in the USA
Charleston, SC
01 December 2015